by Marya Mannes

THEY
BUT WILL IT SELL?
THE NEW YORK I KNOW
MORE IN ANGER
MESSAGE FROM A STRANGER

with Robert Osborn
SUBVERSE: RHYMES FOR OUR TIMES

They

They

a novel by
Marya Mannes

Doubleday & Company, Inc.
Garden City, New York

1968

All of the characters in this book are
fictitious, and any resemblance to actual
persons, living or dead, is purely coin-
cidental.

TO NO ESTABLISHMENT

They

Prologue

California 168359217

Although circumstances have forced me to release my mother's manuscript in its entirety, it is with mixed feelings that I do so for reasons that will be self-evident. But since it has already been circulated in the underground press in the guise of a serious statement, causing ferment and unrest among the younger generation, I have considered it necessary to expose it for what it is.

Two decades ago, in the transitional period of anarchy, it might have been considered by some as a literary attempt. Now, when individual, hence subjective, criticism in all the arts has been supplanted by computer value scales, this account has been established as a clinical document testifying to my mother's particular degenerative, paranoiac condition. In spite of its occasional deceptive lucidity it is clearly the product of a disordered, in fact, hallucinated mind; of value

11

only to psycho-scientists or, as a social and historical curiosity, possibly of interest to those scholars analyzing the "lost world" of the past.

It is for the purpose of placing this document in its right perspective, at a time when the rebellious young have begun to use it as a rallying point against our society, that I reluctantly expose it to general view. Balanced and mature citizens will recognize it for what it is, and in so doing, hopefully help dispel the glamor and mystery surrounding its illegal and unsanctioned disclosure.

The circumstances preceding and following this disclosure are as follows:

As she states, my mother and her friends were given special exemption to live in our former family house rather than in the planned communities which we had established for the old and in which we had hoped to place her. In a structured situation she might have been spared the breakdown which apparently occurred after my father's death and the political and social changes brought about by domestic and international crises. These, together with the death of my younger brother in the Asian war, must have deepened and magnified her sense of isolation and alienation to the point herein evident. She was not, of course, aware of Ben's death, but it is clear that through some form of psychic perception she created in his image the young man she identified as Michael. The physical resemblance to my late brother is close and his "dumbness" can be translated as the inability of her dead son to communicate.

The existence of this manuscript came to my attention first through my elder son, whom I found reading it in one of the several underground papers now circulating on the nation's

12

campuses. This archaic addiction to print is one of the most disturbing factors among young people today. It appears to be a sign of emotional imbalance that has reached serious epidemic proportions in spite of stringent measures to control it. My mother was correct in assuming that communication is now overwhelmingly electronic, the reading of printed words being reduced to subjects of specialized and limited interest.

There is, however, a growing cult—primitive, even religious in nature—which appeals to the alienated young of this day and which, if uncontrolled, may have unforeseen and probably disruptive consequences to our new society.

In any event, my son—who of course had never known his grandmother or the family house—could not identify either the narrator or the other persons involved. The moment I recognized them, of course, I set about immediately to find out how this manuscript—since the persons concerned in it had since died—found its way into other hands and illegal publication.

After a long search I finally came upon a news tape of a year ago making brief mention of an incident on the coast northeast of New York in which a large house—clearly in the location of our old family residence—burned, consuming its inhabitants.

This spectacular blaze was witnessed by the driver of an Agency truck who had come on a routine house call. He immediately radioed for fire equipment. While doing so he thought he saw the silhouette of a tall, thin, bearded youth running out of the burning house with a box or parcel and disappearing into the darkness. This was doubtless the arsonist himself, although why he should have bothered to salvage only this manuscript, which appears to have been the case, has remained as mysterious as his subsequent whereabouts.

Equally mysterious and inexplicable is the final inscription. Not only could my mother not write Latin but the letters were in a hand wholly different from hers or, for that matter, from the normal printing of her time. Scholars claim that their formation corresponds to that of Roman letters at the time of christianity, but again this would not have been in the competence of anyone present in the house. The religious implications are equally mystifying. It seems evident from my mother's account that none of the five were religiously inclined, although, of course, their situation might have forced them back into forgotten molds of faith.

Again, the unfortunate, and unfortunately wide, underground circulation this manuscript has received has made christianity not only a campus fad but a form of escape from the technological rationality that has made our newly structured society what it is today.

We have taken long strides forward. We must not let Them lead us back into the "lost world"—and the long-discredited "values" of humanism.

6B8953A-411-Y

■ It is early April after a night of rain.

I have been to the beach to clear my head and smell the sea and throw things for By.

As I near the house—turreted, shingled, towered, porched—I see Barney digging in the earth with his wheelbarrow near him. He raises his ugly face in what he means as an amiable grimace and I go inside with By.

I hear Lev and Joey practicing their Brahms in the living room, and as I go in Lev stops short, and then Joey stops, and Lev says, "For Christ's sake, Joey! Andante isn't a crawl!"

Joey mutters and they resume. I hang my coat on a peg and go to the kitchen to see what Annie is doing. Phu is lying on the tread of the doorway so that I have to step over him. By decides not to bother and turns instead into my workroom, where he thumps down.

Annie is rolling dough, looks up.

She smiles. "Nice at the beach?"

"Damp, but hope in the air. And a strong clammy smell . . ."

I go into the small room where my desk and By are, and decide that I cannot put it off any longer if I do it at all. And I agree with the others that I must do it if anything is to make any sense at all.

For who are we and where is this place? It could be a house party or a family and it is both and neither. And when I write of we and They and you, as I shall, repeatedly, who am I talking about? More importantly, who am I writing for, since—presumably—nobody reads any more?

Who will care, unless there is some great counter-upheaval after our death or—in Their terms—Regression? For weeks I have been blocked by this heavy weight of futility, even though I have forced myself to take careful notes of what we have said and done since I accepted the task of chronicler.

They chose me because I was, or rather had been, the only writer among us. The job I had had before it happened was as contributing editor of the last big-circulation magazine to exist, and they thought I had a clear head and could make a thorough and orderly record.

Order. Even before They took over, it had become a dirty word, this product of logic, or reason, of the conscious mind. Which is rather ironic because in what They have done there is a great deal of order: cool, considered, relentless. But even before we were put away, all Their forms of expression or communication, or what we used to call "art," denied order on the grounds that it was alien and destructive to the spirit of man. And yet, so rooted are we—that is, those of us who are old enough to have been reared and educated in the classic disciplines—so rooted are we in what we also thought to be the natural, the universal, order of things that we find it almost impossible to express ourselves in any other way. Whether anybody ever reads this or not, I have to write it in—what did that Canadian professor say?—the linear way. Or try to.

You all remember when it began. You see, there it goes again. "You." Who are you? You will obviously be They, since no one else will be alive. It is eerie to have no conception whatever of an audience, no idea of any receiving eye or ear.

Anyway, we should have known long before They actually took over that something of the sort was going to happen, but people never really believe anything until it does happen. In our forties and later we kept reading about how half of all Americans would be twenty-five years old by 1970, and a slight chill would creep over us as we saw our half more and more irrelevant and what we called our "values" less and less pertinent to Them.

And in spite of the mounting emphasis on Them that stamped this period (They set the pace in practically everything), we felt that Their revolution might in time be tempered and modified by Their own maturity. Some of us, as I said, welcomed the climate of social change as inevitable, however disruptive.

After all, age was never the object of veneration or admiration in America, even though we still remembered a time when respect in manners if not in mind was accorded it. And how could we seriously claim that our generation as a whole deserved it? Affluent as it was for the majority, the society we had produced was not admirable. It might be better than others, but it was nowhere near what it should have been. It was, in fact, going rotten.

The private gain had for so long triumphed over the public need that the cities had become unlivable, the country desecrated, the arteries choked, and pollution—of air, of water, yes, of spirit too—a daily, oppressive, fact.

And who else but our generation (if not ourselves) had made it so?

Yet the chill of Their total pre-emption persisted. And although four of us—and when I say us or we I mean our small group in this house—had had successful careers and even national reputations, we were beginning to lose our nerve.

This is about as good a time as any to be specific about ourselves, although I shall leave Michael until the last because he came later and will be the last to go. Before the exile the rest of us were all in our fifties (fifty, of course, was the mandatory age of retirement) and, as I said, fairly successful; except for Barney, who had had the misfortune to reach the crest of his career when he was a young man.

Barney is sixty-four, with a stooped but powerful body and a face like an Epstein head: pitted, gnarled, with a crop of grizzled hair and small deep eyes that can be kind or violent.

Already in his thirties, Barney had been widely admired as a painter in a time when "representational" painting—and his was considerably more than that—was still considered a permissible occupation. Whatever he saw—trees or bodies, faces or lakes, a cluster of berries or a distant barn—he invested with a singular aura, a separate life. Whatever he painted he not only knew but loved, as he loved the quality of paint itself. It was a sensuous act, both spontaneous and deliberate, organized and free. His passion for life and his passion for his craft were self-evident and interdependent. He was of no school although he acknowledged many masters.

[18]

But although his paintings hung in many museums and in the rooms of many private collectors, the reviews of his last show—what year was it?—and the climate of the time confirmed what he had long begun to suspect: he was overtaken. Overtaken by a new breed, a new vision, new hungers for shock and novelty, for size and primitivism, which he was unable to feed. He saw the arrogant amateur proclaimed king in a court of what he called ball-less fools, and he read his own death sentence.

So, although nearly all his paintings in this last show were sold and one critic gave him a splendid obituary, Barney never touched a brush or canvas again. He started drinking heavily, and Annie was saddled for years before the exile with a man who did little but curse and putter, stupefied with rage. All he appeared to love were Annie and Trilling, a bird they got just before they were put away. I asked them why they named it after the late critic, but since neither of them had read or known him, it became obvious that it just described what he did. The bird, I mean.

What Barney has retained from his past disciplines as an artist is a sense of form and a manual dexterity that has made him a superb carpenter and general handyman. I don't know how we could have survived these years in this place without his skill and—however difficult at times—his fury. Adrenalin can apparently be as life-giving as hormones.

Annie is a year younger than Barney. She must have had the body of a Maillol woman when she was his model and mistress. (You see how impossible all this is: what can *you* be expected to know about names like Epstein and Maillol since They cut off even this recent past? What can they mean to you, since even before They took over, our young were looking blank at mention of artists and writers well-known even during the thirties of this century? What possible frame of reference can I use that you can share?)

No matter. Let's say that Annie is unmistakably of the Ukrainian peasant stock of her origins: broad face, high cheek-bones, button nose, and still (here we go again) the Renoir skin that Barney must have doted on. Now her heavy breasts have merged with her stomach and she does not care how she looks. But she has an intuitive intelligence and an encompassing warmth for all living things except Phu. She is also, thank God or accident, an inspired and compulsive cook. She would have to be, for except for what we grow in summer, our allowances keep us to a very simple, and increasingly Spartan, diet.

Joey, a year younger than Barney, was one of the most popular song writers for Broadway musicals in his day: a master of the lyric phrase that lifted the breath and touched the heart before both were lost in a tangle of sonic tape beyond reach of the human voice. Do any of you know any of his songs? Would they move you?

Joey looks like a cross between a rhesus monkey and the mad doctor in an old horror movie, but that had not prevented him from being irresistible to women, for whom he had a tireless and not always discriminating passion.

Lev, now in his early sixties, had been one of our major conductors. This you must know of him, because even They didn't question his scrupulous musicianship. He was, as so many musicians had been, a naturalized Austrian Jew, with his musical roots in Berlin and Vienna and certain characteristics (apart from his ineradicable accent) shared by this intellectual emigration from Middle Europe as a whole. Chief of these was the assumption, sometimes justified, of cultural superiority.

Stiffly erect, his graying hair receding in a peak from his big high forehead, his nose strong and his eyes hooded, he was an imperious figure on and off stage. His boundless ego was matched only by his humility toward music. His vanity could be tiresome if his wit had not leavened it. He had been married for thirty years to a French woman who bore him two daughters and whom he divorced for Lily, who is no longer with us.

As for me, I am the mother of two sons whom I have not seen for over ten years (as Lev has not seen his daughters, or Joey his twins), the grandmother of a girl and a boy whom I have never seen, and the widow of a man I loved. It is hard to describe myself. They tell me I look much younger than I am. I used to be beautiful and I guess the bones are still there, although my hair is graying and my skin dry. But these degenerations which we all now share are somehow less hurtful without Their presence as reminder. Besides, we work very hard at keeping alive; and strong.

There are three animals in his asylum.

There is my black retriever, slightly gray at the muzzle, called Bayard, or By (and he *is* without fear or reproach).

There is Phu, a male Siamese belonging to Lev and named after one of those little Asian military dictators we always used to back: sleek and arrogant and devious. We tell Lev that the name is unfair because the cat is above all independent, which is more than one could have said of his namesake.

The noble By gets along with everybody, but Phu is a problem with the bird. He sits and eyes Trilling in his cage with demonic intensity and Annie is in constant dread that he will get a paw in or knock the cage open when no one is looking. To add insult to this premise of injury, Phu, with the unerring instinct for people who don't like cats, keeps running against her legs or leaping into her lap while Lev laughs and Annie shouts and Phu, shoved down, walks away with his tail at full mast making crude whining comments.

So this is who we were, before Michael came. Obviously, the next question I must answer (why "must"?; and for whom?) is how we got here. The trouble is that there were so many contributory and converging reasons for the beginning of it all that it's hard to know where to start, and impossible to know how much of it all *you* really know after a decade or so of virtual quarantine from the truth as we think it and live it.

During the first year together here we talked of very little else: how did it start? When did each of us first feel its imminence? What was the specific nature of this chill I keep talking about? I have tried to make a brief synthesis of these conversations:

JOEY: I think it was when a kid came to audition for me chewing gum (she had great boobs, but why do these kids spend an hour on their face and then chew gum?) and I was telling her to try and put in this song the kind of feeling in Kern's "Just My Bill," and she says, "Who?" Oh, hell, it was a lot of things.

It was hearing my songs used as commercial jingles to sell cars or soft drinks, it was the dirty lyrics sung by dirty bums, it was going to a show that was made of four-letter words and repulsive people and then reading next day how great it was, how "significant." It was a lot of rank amateurs making it overnight.

It was ape-talk.

BARNEY: I'd rather have ape-talk than double-talk. The

whole stinking farce began right after the Second World War when supposedly serious art magazines began printing this farting fag double-talk, you know, they show this canvas with one ball (would be one ball) down on the left and a sort of line wiggling off right, and you know what that is? It's "a sense of spacial function in which kinetic elements arrive at their own synthesis!"

LEV: I think I first got the chill when this wife of one of our new young symphony trustees—you know, they were the so-called Beautiful People, terribly chic and In—well she came up to me at a party and said couldn't I play some of the "fun pieces" of our new young American composers, and I said like what, and she said, oh those fascinating things with tape and weird noises, didn't I think they were a breakthrough into the new composition?

She was completely serious, and I told her I spent my life looking for new compositions with something to say to the heart as well as to the mind, but that unfortunately I was usually faced with a choice between aural rape and deadly monotony, and I did not want to put my musicians or my audience through either. But I knew where the wind was blowing, and that last season before . . . to so speak . . . I was retired and they hired a boy genius to conduct, I decided to blast my subscribers' ears off with two electronic masturbations and got an accolade in the press for "at last recognizing new thresholds of sound!"

"Hey!" said Joey, "I think I heard one—it sounded like a swarm of mosquitoes and a guy scratching his bites!"

"That is right," said Lev.

ANNIE: I remember that for the first time in my life I was afraid of the young. I was afraid of them in groups, like when

[23]

they came out of high school at three, they were so tough and hard and dirty-mouthed. And then . . . then I couldn't find any dress to fit me. They were all for little girls. . . .

I agreed with Annie. I thought if I saw any more pictures of teen-age girls, I would die. . . . And I remember when our new editor took me aside one day and said that "we must orient the magazine more to the young market." Our image was "too mature."

I also said that I couldn't understand the homework Sam and Ben brought home. And later, when Sam became a physicist, I couldn't understand anything he and his friends talked about. It was, simply, a new language.

Joey remembered something more. "I read a piece in some paper about East Village and the life there, and some young painter in a slum tenement there said, 'For this generation, history is about ten seconds ago.'"

We agreed that this about wrapped it up.

But these were just the distant mutterings before the close, splitting, claps of thunder. When They began taking over the Universities, not only here but in the other civilized capitals of the world, the sign was scratched in lightning.

Oh, we rationalized what we saw as much as we could. The institutions they attacked were cumbersome and unresponsive, slow—as all institutions are—to change. Lev was constantly railing at the inhumanity of mass education, at the fundamental illiteracy he claimed it produced. All of us were as outraged at the Vietnam war of the sixties as They were, as our own sons were. If Ben had burned his draft card (he said he didn't have the guts to do it), Jeff and I would have backed him up. There was not one of us here who had not known young people of brilliance, compassion, and honor, or who did not salute their insistence on new goals in revulsion against the corporate materialism and political cynicism of the old ones.

But when the militants took over—hostile and incoherent, contemptuous of law, using force (as the only tool of the spiritually illiterate), screaming against the counter-force they brought on them—every instinct in us froze.

This was another breed; a totalitarian breed. And from them we could expect no quarter.

■ Today there's a fierce wind blowing from the north, but I had to get some air.

I walked to the beach with By, buffeted from behind by the gusts that swept over the still-frozen fields and bent the high reeds that fringed one side of the pond. By made several bounding forays into them, head snuffling earth, tail high, but if there had indeed been a rabbit, there was none now. He turned back to me looking slightly sheepish and then trotted ahead of me onto the wide beach.

The sea was roiled and angry, the color a sullen greenish gray, the tops of the jostling, perverse waves blown back in high froth. We turned eastward, the low dunes giving us only slight shield from the cutting wind.

The beach seemed bare except for a ring of wet pebbles at the tide mark, some dry seaweed farther up, and a few pieces of wood. But then, long before we were isolated, I had noticed that the ocean was giving back less and less of its own and more and more of ours. By that I mean that cans and cartons and plastic bottles and light bulbs—the indestructible litter of our life—were gradually replacing the moon shells and starfish and mussels and quahogs of earlier days. It seemed almost like a backhanded slap from the mighty element: "Okay you rats, why should I send you miracles any more when you defile my waters? Take *this*—and *this*—and *this*. It's all yours!"

There were still rare moments when you came suddenly upon the marvelous internal spiral of a conch, or a moon shell in subtle browns and blacks, or a huge clam shell with a handsome blue cartographical pattern on its interior surface. Barney and I would gather them up and take them back until bowl after bowl and shelf after shelf were full of them and we had to weed out the less good every few months and find the better again. Or what seemed the better when we came upon them.

By was looking at me reproachfully, so I picked up a piece of wet wood, went nearer the water, and threw it straight into the surf. In great black shining bounds he plunged into the froth, paddled until he got it in jaws, scrabbled out, and brought it almost to me, shaking the sea from himself. The usual ritual followed. "Drop it, By! Give it to me!" You know, surely. It has to be done that way. He twitches it away from my hand until I pretend to lose interest and then he drops it on the sand until I am about to grab it and then he takes it, and so forth. Sometimes there's a hand-and-mouth tussle until the time for surrender, without which, of course, he knows it can't be thrown again.

After three of these games as we walk along, my eyes to the sand, I see about twenty yards away something that turns out to be what I think it must be: a dead animal. The tiny tracks of the feet of other birds lead up to it and circle around it like a wreath of curiosity or deference. It should deserve the latter. For although a gull in life (handsome as it may be arcing in air) is on land a crude and clumsy garbage eater, selfish and querulous, a gull in death has surprising sanctity.

This one, pure white and big as a goose, lay on its back, its head to one side, its breast uncorrupted, its wings hugging its body like a shroud . . . or like the swaddling clothes of a Della Robbia child. (*Who*, you say?)

It was a thing wholly of peace and beauty, and I found myself wishing we looked like that when we died, in natural grace and order.

By gave a perfunctory look and galloped down to the water. I followed him to where the pebbles were and walked along, looking, looking.

For what? For a miracle, always. For perfection, I suppose. The perfect form, the ultimate shape. So many of them almost had it. I would pick them up and feel them, turning them over and over between my fingers, loving the cold, the smoothness, the infinite subtlety of surface; worshiping the whiteness or the blackness or the pigeon-heart coral or the saffron yellow, so many of which turned gray or brown or ochre when they dried. What was magical about them? I kept wondering. Why were they always a renewal? And of what?

■ I was writing about the convergence of many things, the first one being the chill, the premonition of removal. It was as if there were a ship leaving a pier, and we did not know whether we were the ship or the pier, or if we were the ship, where it was going, or if we were the pier, on what shore we were left.

We would go to exhibitions of new art, and not understand

or, worse, be moved by most of what we saw. Others called it significant and important, but we saw brutality and chaos, arrogance or frivolity, fashion or incompetence.

We would read a book that others reviewed as brilliant and find it self-indulgent gibberish or pretentious symbolism. We could not even understand the reviews.

We would go to plays celebrating evil with four-letter words or stuttering nothing, and come away empty. There was no heart in these things.

We kept looking for meaning, for standards, for order (those stones, those shells, that gull) and were told they were no longer relevant. (Joey remembered a prominent critic saying of a certain play that "because it means nothing is surely not important . . ." and later describing it as "nothing but a pattern of forces, a pattern of abstract sensory signals."

We were told daily that mind (logic, reason) meant nothing and that only sensation counted.

Words were of no importance, except to the intellectual arbiters who used them to tell us this.

And the man who told us that writing was dead could not write.

■ They were always looking over my shoulder to see how I was getting on, or snitching looks when I was out of the room. I begged them not to and sometimes tried to hide the typescript, but gave up in the end. Anyway, it was their story even if they had insisted I write it, so what they became in fact was a sort of rotating editorial board whose marginal comments (when coherent) I have tried to include.

[28]

Joey has just come in. He put his hand down my shirt and said "Nice!" and kept it there while he read.

"Don't forget," he said, "that a lot of this sort of crap was pushed on the public by people old enough to know better. Don't blame Them if Their mini-talents were blown up out of all proportion. The cultural elite was so goddamn scared of missing the boat they'd ride on junk."

"Another thing," he said, "there *were* real talents. The folk singers and combos. Some of the songs and ballads those pop groups sang were great."

"The new troubadours," I said. "Yes—they cared . . ."

I confessed I was crazy about the beat and sad and jealous that I could not shake and twist and weave to it, with long hair flying, as They did. To love dance and not be of it hurt—most painfully.

"Anyway," said Joey, giving a final pat before he pulled his hand out, "They did a lot for sex and Their clothes were great. Those girls with their long hair and their long legs disturbed hell out of me."

I told him that a girl could be muffled head to foot and disturb hell out of him and he grinned happily. "Even old bags," he shot in my direction as he left.

■ (*Note from Barney*)

If we're going to be kind to the little bastards, I'll second Joey. They looked great except for the girls with bad legs and no tits.

But I guess you find those anytime.

Me I like more flesh.

■ We got back to the chills, the widening gap, that evening by the fire.

JOEY: The producer of my last show threw a party for the cast on closing night. They were all kids so he took over the go-go joint that was hottest that year and the kids insisted on taking me along.

After a half hour in that hellhole, I couldn't take it. The noise was so deafening I thought my eardrums would burst, the goddamn psychedelic lights made my stomach heave. The whole thing was a violent bludgeoning of the senses, and I thought, Christ, if this is what people need to turn 'em on, good-bye world.

LEV: It is They who said good-bye first.

JOEY: Okay, okay, but the point is that I've seen a lot of changes in my life, I've batted around more than most, and by God I never before had this feeling that I didn't belong any more, that I was on Mars. It scared the hell out of me.

LEV: I agree with Joey about the extent of the gap. It was something much more than the usual thing between generations. I was impatient with my parents for many reasons, I too rebelled in my youth, but I did not think of them as another race, did you, Kate?

K: No. Just slow to understand, maybe.

ANNIE: Sometimes I hated my mother . . .

BARNEY: Hate! Hate! Hell, that's a lot better than what *They* felt about us—if they felt anything it was contempt, but most of the time we didn't exist, we were *dead* before we died!

LEV: Of course, because only the present exists for them, they are the children of Now.

This is the sort of talk that went on week after week in the years of our exile, from the first months of incredulous shock to this terminal period of balance and a measure of peace. It was Them—always Them.

Why we should have been shocked by Their formal takeover after the years of Their de facto dominance, I do not know. Those of then in our fifties would never forget the bombardment of sight and sound, the barrage of contempt, that so relentlessly demeaned us, stripped us of our worth, ignored our existence.

Day after day we could not pick up a paper or a magazine without the faces of youth, flawless, unformed, tossing their swinging shining hair at us and striding with their long childish legs across the pages and screens of our lives. Younger and younger they became, strutting and laughing, swigging their soft drinks, dancing in their kaleidoscopes of color, nearly naked or clad in dolls' clothes, booted, spurred, armed, triumphant.

Older men, once handsome and secure in their gray or receding hair, dyed it or bought themselves toupees.

Older women hiked their skirts above their knobby knees and had silicone pumped into their breasts or faces. To dress (unless they were rich enough to command their style) they were forced to dress like dolls because no clothes were made for women. The word had become obsolete: it implied maturity. (Barney put a red line through this and wrote "dirty"!)

"You know," said Joey once, "in that last year outside I only remember one commercial with somebody old in it. She was constipated."

"Irregular," I said.

[31]

Like the Negroes, whose sin was color, ours was age. The punishment was indifference or contempt, and both meant exclusion from the mainstream of living.

But was our sin only age? we asked ourselves over and over.

Was it our fault, not Theirs? In our forties and fifties were we already gripped by spiritual arteriosclerosis? A hardening of the arteries of perception that blinded us to the new? Was everything that we had believed and loved invalid and irrelevant in the light of matter exploded and re-formed into wholly new patterns? Were They on the edge of a revelation our age denied us?

Or was there—could there be coming, in the midst of the greatest technological leap known to man, the mastery of his universe—a night of the soul, a return to a new form of barbarism?

For you see, it wasn't only Their doing, although perhaps I should have made it more clear that They applies not only to the young. The machines were part of the takeover, for they had invaded every function of daily life.

The punch card was the passport to living. This we had learned to accept as inevitable, but it was part of the general chill. It was also a damnable nuisance to a generation used to direct personal contact, to human, as against mechanical, service; a service, I must add, not to the consumer but to the corporation.

We were told, of course, that the machine was still the servant of the man: that what you put into it determined what came out of it. And the simple fact was that when the programmers, in their new, special, and, to us, totally incomprehensible language, fed their machines the plethora of data available on the old, out came the one recurrent and irrefutable answer: dispensable. And it was the machine that planned every detail of our exile and disposition and now controls our precisely limited future.

■ Joey had a look at these last pages and said I ought to say more about not knocking the kids for all the things that estranged us, that there were good things going on in that time and that the bad things—or what we called bad—were the work of an "in" group, a self-appointed cultural establishment, well in their forties or over. And the advertisers and editors and TV people who blew the kids up all out of proportion.

He said we ought to be more specific about it, and I think he's right. So I told the others after dinner that they ought to think about it and try not to be negative.

Barney gave a loud belch and Annie turned on him and said, "She is right. Don't be such a baby." Lev said nothing. I said that if they didn't want to talk about it, then just write about it.

They looked apathetic and changed the subject, but the next day, to my surprise, I found on my desk some pages scribbled in characteristic bravura from Barney.

"Sure there was some good stuff around," he wrote, "a lot of painters knew how to sock you in the eye, they knew about color, they knew about light, they put their guts on canvas. But most of them didn't really get any further than shock or decoration. You got it all in one wallop, there just wasn't anything more to it. The movies were better."

"Now, a few had mystery. Pollock was one of them, and there were others. They had a *richness*. But most of the paintslingers were *thin*—not enough—nothing *inside*. Just a goddam poverty. Poverty and arrogance."

"Part of that was this business of not looking outside—not seeing anything but their crummy selves. Most of them had no humility before the *fact*. Hell no, don't paint anything you *see,* that's dead. Paint what you *feel*. Why the hell didn't they look at land from an airplane or germs through a microscope? Better goddamn patterns than those shits could dream up! But no, that's *real*, that doesn't count—back to the navel, boys, and psych yourself."

"As for Pop—that was great. Great for Madison Avenue and penthouse idiots."

"The sculptors were on the whole much better. I don't mean those junkmen or auto wreckers and I don't mean those bastards who put painted pieces of nothing in the park. I mean the artisans who had respect for stone, respect for steel, for pure form. They cut out the crap and got down to universal basics— the curve, the organic shapes."

"But for Christ's sake, don't get me wrong—95.1 per cent of what they called art was crap, and I'll stick with it."

Although this had very little to do with Them—most of what Barney was damning was the work of their elders—I thanked him profusely for his trouble, shaming Lev into writing the following. (As usual in his small impeccable script.)

"Don't show this to Joey," he wrote, "because it will make him even more intolerable than usual, but if you ask me what was good in music in those days—those years of the sixties—I would say folk music. By that I mean show music, popular music, entertainment music rather than 'serious' music, for concert repertoires. This has always been the great American contribution. I cannot remember with deep pleasure any 'serious' American score composed in that last particular decade, although of course I conducted the best I could find."

"I think I would agree with Barney about the thinness, the lack of content, not to speak of real style. They did not create, they embroidered in sound. At best this music could be used as a sound track for films. At worst it was an infection of the ear."

"But the songs some of the young people sang with their guitars, that was different. That was music, and it was human."

"Even so, there was nothing even in the popular field to compare with Gershwin or Kern or Rodgers or Cole Porter or Lerner. For, you see, the joy (I am speaking of joy, not fun) was going out of life, and there cannot be song without joy."

■ Trilling is at it again. It's tough to concentrate when he's singing, but it's worse when he's not. He's been silent for two days and we've all been worrying about him.

I found Annie and Lev and Joey hovering over his cage while the bird, beak up and tiny yellow throat pulsing, gave forth his full and umpremeditated song.

"What started him?"

"Well," said Lev, "Vivaldi didn't work, and neither did Mozart. So I thought I'd try 'L'Après-midi' for a change. I whistled the opening, and that did it."

"But he never went for Debussy, we tried . . ."

Joey shrugged. "He's catching up. We're finally dragging him tail first into the nineteenth century."

Trilling has for years responded only to eighteenth-century music. He hates Wagner, ignores Brahms, and jazz or rock make him lie on the floor of his cage with his feet up. We tried Stravinsky once and he started pulling all the feathers out of his breast, so we had to stop it.

[35]

Usually he starts singing on his own, but when he's depressed nothing will trigger him off except the crystalline cadences and limpid patterns of the eighteenth century.

"Too bad his improvisation is so limited," said Lev. "Otherwise we could have trios. Strange how such an essentially unmusical little organism can have such taste."

"God help the little bastard if we played him some Cage," said Joey.

Funny. None of us three are bird people, but this "little organism" has become part of our lives. Why? Because he shares our hunger for clarity? For design?

■ The strange musical coupling of a popular song writer and a renowned conductor both fascinated and confounded us. It also saved us.

It was born of necessity—the imperative need of musicians to make music—and made providentially possible by the presence of an old Steinway grand that belonged to Jeff's mother and had remained largely mute since she played it. It stood in an alcove beyond, but in clear sight of, the living room.

From the moment he came here, Lev worked with passionate intensity to restore it. Long disuse and damp sea winds had put it out of tune, and a number of keys and hammers were barely functioning. With Barney's manual dexterity and the tuning fork that was Lev's unerring ear, the piano gradually came to life again. The rebirth was painful to the rest of us, as anyone familiar with tuning will know, but the first time Lev really let go on it was a triumphant and moving moment.

The trouble came when, like birds at a feeder, Lev and

Joey started pushing each other off the piano stool, and during the first months the feeling between the two men ran high.

We recognized Lev's claim to priority: his musical stature warranted it even if his resurrection of the instrument had not reinforced it.

But Joey's addiction to the keyboard was equally natural. It was the extension of his ears and fingers, the inseparable playmate of his invention. Lev had other resources, Joey none.

Even without real knowledge of music, I grew to understand Lev's annoyance with Joey's largely untutored facility, his slick improvisations, his genial carelessness even when they gave the rest of us pleasure and release. Lev's European traditions made him profoundly contemptuous of easy pleasures even when he would admit Joey's lyrical talent.

But when Joey would try his hands at classic compositions, slurring the fast passages and luxuriating sentimentally in the slow ones, Lev exploded. There were ugly scenes followed by protracted estrangements, and the atmosphere in the house grew so tense that something had to be done. Like a swimming pool, the use of the piano was carefully scheduled between the two men, with the hours posted on the music rack.

But as time went on this proved not only unworkable but preposterous. Instead, the teacher in Lev triumphed. He would take Joey in hand and tell him how to play the piano. This was not as altruistic as it might sound, for Lev said it would save his sanity if Joey learned how to play, and anyway they could branch out to duets, of which more later.

I must say, Joey took to this with surprising humility. He knew, as he often told me, how little he knew. He said he had enormous respect for "that bastard," and anyway what could he lose?

Once in authority, his native climate, Lev became an inspired and devoted teacher. He shouted at Joey repeatedly but was quick to beam encouragement when he improved.

Since I could not possibly write during their "lessons," I began more and more to listen to them, first invisible on the porch when weather permitted, and later—with their first reluctant consent—from the adjoining room, where I could look at them play.

I learned then at close range what music did to musicians. Their faces change. They enter a new dimension, something I found very close to what I imagined as religious experience. It was the immersion of self in a larger and deeper element. Lev's arrogant features seemed to grow softer, and Joey's tough and worldly face took on a surprising spirituality. They were clearly in something bigger than themselves of which love—an abstract and yet deeply organic love—was the source.

I had often felt this love at concerts of great music, this—this enlargement of aspiration, this total rejection of the mean, the small, the inconsequential in the face of grandeur and truth. Or, if you will, the grandeur of truth made manifest in man. I was filled with understanding and compassion for all things, and would—listening—be willing to die for them.

But here, close at hand, it was predominantly life that these two brought to the house: the life inside to supplant the life outside.

■ (*Note from Lev*)

My dear Kate, this is all very flattering but somewhat embarrassing. Believe me we are not thinking of truth or grandeur, we are worring about fingering and pitch and what is for dinner.

That noble look you refer to (Joey *noble?*) is merely concentration.

(*Me to Lev*)
I didn't say "noble," I said "spiritual."

(*Lev—later*)
Even worse.

■ That Canadian *was* right: you can't be linear. Everything is a convergence, and no more so than the meeting of forces in that one word Them, or They.

For what really brought the sense of crisis that followed the chill was not merely domination by the young or by the machine but the brief return to political power of a reactionary coalition under a conservative President.

This was the result of the last election before our exile, and it appalled us considerably more than what They were doing.

Actually, what They were doing precipitated the choice. A public fed up with civil disruption, blatant defiance of law, and violent racial trouble, rose in great numbers to the cry of "Law and Order!" The man who promised to end "crime in the streets" won over the men who hoped to attack its cause. Not in any landslide, but with enough margin to perpetuate—or at least try to—old simplistic concepts of "American values." What won was the very thing They most abhorred: the military-industrial complex, the massive use of force against civil disorder of whatever origin or reason, and the same old

Congress responsible—through blindness and lethargy—for its existence.

To this, of course, was added the "patriots'" cry of anti-Communism (public impatience with endless negotiations gave this fuel) and the resumption of a "stronger hand" in Asia.

But why should I tell you this—you who are They?

You know it all, although you choose to forget that many of us were as outraged as you were when this archaic group came into power. The trouble was that neither we nor you had realized the extent of their support, nor the national hunger for simple and violent solutions to problems neither could solve. The gun-people won.

■ So, one day we read on the front pages of our one remaining newspaper that our air force had made a preemptive nuclear attack on a Chinese missile site. With horror we saw what we had consistently dreaded: another giant, possibly fatal, step in the steadily intensified war waged by a new administration even more obdurate than its predecessor in its insistence on "victory."

Barney came in at this moment.

"Have a look at this, Kate," he said, and handed me a flawlessly smooth black stone the size of his palm, shaped, with incredible subtlety of grading, like the flanges of a propeller.

"Ever felt anything more marvelous?" he asked. "Christ, *that's* abstraction, *that's* sensual revelation for you! Why don't those piddling bastards who call themselves sculptors look at things like *that* instead of banging together tractor parts ten feet high and painting them shit-yellow!"

It was a familiar speech.

"Brancusi knew it—Arp knew it—hell, the Japs know it. But not the fancy boys at the fancy shows, *they* don't look at anything but their cruddy navels!"

"It's beautiful," I said, handing it back to him. He bent over to look at what I had written. He smelled of earth and sweat, which was not unpleasing even though I wished he would wash more than once a week.

"Why are you so goddamned polite about those bastards?"

"I didn't think I was."

Barney snorted. "Why don't you call them the Lunatic Right? Why don't you say they've always been more dangerous to this country than the commies?"

"Barney, it's clear enough. I'm just trying to explain what happened—how one thing followed another."

He grunted and left. I must say I found his old-line liberalism rather endearing. I was only surprised that he didn't use "fascist beasts."

But they weren't, really. They were merely stupid, and that was dangerous enough.

■ In any event, the possible imminence of nuclear retaliation forced the nation into a massive civil defense system that put it on a virtually martial basis. Even before that a great many underground community shelters had been quietly constructed, not only in the major urban centers but in isolated areas, using existent caves as bases for wider excavation.

The first we knew about these were in little newspaper items in different parts of the country that went like this:

"A network of man-made caves here that have been used

[41]

for mushroom cultivation are being transformed into subterranean sanctuaries to store securities and works of art." It mentioned a certain storage company that had acquired a ninety-nine-year lease on the caves, which stretched beneath thirty-two acres of hills in New York State. In addition to storing valuable documents and works of art, this item went on, "the vault would provide space for the establishment of corporate management headquarters if New York City, ninety miles to the south, had to be evacuated in wartime."

These items always sent a premonitory shudder through us which was quickly forgotten in the day's work and the patterns of living. We did not think of them again until They marshaled Their force for the coming elections.

Violently antiwar, sick (as we were) of martial adventures described as democratic benediction, appalled at renewed racial violence, They finally got themselves together in a unified national organization and started to draw plans for the takeover at the next elections.

I have oversimplified this, because you must know all the details and the only thing I can add is how *we*—your parents, your grandparents—reacted to what you believed you had to do. For since you cut us off entirely from the mainstream—your stream—how can you know what went on in this exile—as long as it lasted for each of us?

As I said before, many of us were as sickened by what was happening during that brief "conservative" interregnum as you were. You were essentially right in believing that what was holding back this country from the course it should take was the resistance of the older political generation to necessary and radical change, although you conveniently forgot that some

[42]

of the bravest opponents of the new-old government were over sixty. Still you knew that too many of this aging generation had memories of older days, nostalgia for older ways, and a gnawing, if unassuageable, hunger for values which you had proved so ably to yourselves were dead. We were all that was left of the first half of the twentieth century, all that was impeding the twenty-first. So was the heritage in which we grew up.

So what began as the protection of this heritage from the threat of atomic war ended, after your election to power, in its burial in the sealed caves and caverns of our various states. Outright destruction would, of course, have encountered too great and powerful a reaction. But this—this steady, quiet withdrawal of all the documents and works of art in this country created before the second half of the twentieth century —was simply a "defense measure," reverentially carried out by our new caretakers. We didn't realize what had actually happened until, the war threat ostensibly over for the moment, none of these documents or works of art returned to public accessibility.

And so, with nuclear war still possible if not imminent, the nation remained on a semimartial footing, which managed to convince others, if not ourselves, that our parallel exile was basically for the "protection" of the old; as the segregation of the cultural heritage was the "protection" of the past.

■ Memory—ah, that was the catch. You could remove, bodily, the infections of this past, the ideas and dreams and images and testaments that had dominated Western civilization for centuries—you could do that, and They did. But what could you do with living memory so long as the possessor lived?

You could remove *that* infection by making it inaccessible to the young, and that is exactly what They did.

This segregation had already advanced quite far without Their help. Already those of us in our middle age had noticed (that chill) what was happening to the old in this country. Not only were they accorded neither credence nor dignity; they were simply left to die in a variety of ways, some expensive, some cheap.

The poor, useless, or, more accurately, intolerably burdensome to their children were syphoned off into dingy furnished rooms until they were too feeble to rise from their beds to turn on the television set or put out their garbage. Or they were put, at the first faltering of mind or dribbling of mouth, into institutions of bleak horror where they died by inches in bare corridors looking at nothing.

Or they were put in "nursing" homes attended by slatterns who slapped them when they cried for help and left full bedpans in their beds for half a day.

Or, used for so many years to their little grubby shelters in old tenements, they were evicted (relocated was the word) to make way for some huge white battlement of luxury apartments and put in an alien place, rootless and lost.

Were the rich much better? Oh, much, much better.

They were kept alive at crushing expense and guilt. (*"We couldn't have them live with us, there was no room, you see, and anyway. . . ."*)

Kept alive:

By a paid companion: "Now eat your soup, dear, that's it —we've got to keep our strength, haven't we?

[44]

"Oh, oh, I guess we spilled a little on our nice suit, we mustn't do that, must we?"

By nursing homes at $1500 a month, for only nice people. You visited them once in a while and it all looked very comfortable and clean, except for that special smell of age in the air, that close, dead smell. And your mother, who was seventy-five and very intelligent, said, "It's so wonderful to see you, there are so many old people here, I find them so boring!" And that unbearable parting: "When are you coming again?"

By doctors. Those who were not allowed to die, who were vegetables fed by tubes, who were bodies without minds, or— infinitely worse—minds without bodies, or at least bodies that could function as bodies. Kept alive by the miracles of science, while their eyes looked out of their speechless heads begging to die, to be left alone, to leave the intolerable shell. Yet we were not permitted to kill unwanted life, at either end—at birth or death—until They came.

■ (*Left by Joey*)

Sing a song for Mother's Day,
    Pipe a tune for Dad,
Leave 'em rottin' where they lay
    So long it's not your pad.

Ain't no room for Mom and Dad,
    No room at the inn,
Ain't it awful, ain't it sad
    Thinkin' of your kin?

■ I have forgotten just when Lev started to play his flute again. I didn't even know he had one until I came back to the house one day and heard this pure and lovely sound.

There was Lev with the instrument at his mouth. He removed it when he saw me pause at the door.

"You did not know?" he said with a mischievous and superior smile, "of my early passion?"

"Not this one!"

He told me that he had played it in his youth because he liked the tone, but piano quickly took precedence until conducting superseded it, except for occasional relaxation and accompanying a singer in a coaching session.

"I now intend to resurrect it," he said, "so that Joey and I can expand our repertoire. It is of course highly unorthodox, but I have scores here of many songs and sonatas and—*faute de mieux*—I plan to make the flute double for voice and violin."

"But the piano . . . ?"

"I have spoken to Joey," said Lev, "and I think he can do it—in his own primitive way, of course. But lieder accompaniment should not be beyond him now, and I plan to work him hard—*very* hard—on the sonata literature."

My heart bled for Joey, who confessed later that he was scared but game. He had to be. The first weeks of this new duo were full of tantrums about tempi and interpretation. Wrangle and insults would compete with the notes, and even when I couldn't hear their words I knew that at a given point Joey would walk off telling Lev to go fuck himself, and Lev would retire to his room to talk with Phu.

But once a week, as part of our self-imposed routine, we would gather in the living room and the two would perform for us. Lev would put on his dinner coat and Joey his tie, and we would sit there listening, lost in admiration and lavish with applause.

The two would rise and bow and bow again, and Lev would shake Joey's hands and that was Sunday nights at the Home for Old Folks.

■ Lev asked me to insert the following comment:

In case any musicians or music critics (if there are any left) should read this or any future passages concerning music, I would like to make it clear that our otherwise intelligent house-mistress knows absolutely nothing about music. Neither, for that matter, does anyone else here with the possible exception of Joey, who is one of those childlike natural talents.

I am, however, trying to teach them the rudiments of this noble art so that they will at least understand something of what they hear.

In so doing, unfortunately, I must descend to their level by speaking in oversimplifications.

Nothing else would get through.

■ We all thought this insufferably stuffy, but then that's the central European coming through or, in Lev's words, "get-ing through."

Before this musical interlude I was trying to describe the

plight of the old before their exile, and I realize that I hadn't yet mentioned the gayer alternatives open to "senior citizens" before They took over.

The relatively healthy and well-to-do could spend the last ten or twenty years of their lives in communities of their kind, with all the conveniences, and fun and games. They were called "Leisure-ville" and things like that, and we kept seeing pictures of the "golden-agers" flashing their dentures in the sun and playing shuffleboard or bridge. This made their children very happy, for the old ones were off their necks and enjoying themselves. But some of us wondered how, after involvement in the world, one could be happy having no part in it.

Yet at the same time that all these different and separate visions of hell confronted us middle-aged, other things were happening to make them recede; to keep us, quite simply, from aging.

Some of us were using them long before the exile: hormones, face surgery, special exercises and treatments, all the new techniques for preserving muscle and tissue, organ and bone. At forty-five I looked and felt thirty, and so on. In fact all those who loved life, who were sensuously and sensually aware, were using them and were able, in the first years of Their new administration, to pass as being within the official age limit until a massive search in the government computer data of birth records and passports revealed our actual years.

Of our own group, Barney couldn't have cared less how old he looked; he had Annie and Annie couldn't have fooled him even if she wanted to, which she didn't. As for Joey, he could and did get any woman he wanted at any age so why bother?

[48]

Lev, of course, was a vain man and very conscious of his appearance, as most conductors are in their highly exposed position. Or, in fact, like most public performers, charged as they are by that two-way transmission of vitality between themselves and the audience which acts as a recurrent stimulant. One would have thought that the absence of this audience would withdraw this charge, and in that first difficult year of exile it did. But as you will see, the kind of isolation we were forced into together had its own peculiar compensations with which They had not bargained.

Anyway, there was this large segment of the population now physically as well as spiritually isolated from the young (when, at any time, were the generations further apart even when they lived together?) which would not, or could not, die. Since they were in the main unproductive, draining the government of funds and facilities sorely needed for Their purposes in building a new society, they were, as the machines spelled out, dispensable. Nobody needed them: not their children, not their grandchildren (They thought), not the culture, not the economy. In the event of nuclear war they would be beyond the help of any civil defense system and bound to die a death even more horrible than their slow, sad, and medically protracted ebbing.

And if war did not come, they would still—with their memory of ways and values wholly at variance with current realities—constitute a major obstacle to the building of a pragmatic society strong enough to withstand the enormous pressures—global, cosmic, psychic, what you will—that threatened modern man.

Does this sound cruel to anyone now? It shouldn't. Not in the light of the bursting planet They inherited. For rational beings it was hard to argue against Their premise that it was not life, but the quality of life, that determined its value.

The hitch was, how was that quality determined? They judged it largely in terms of usefulness, and that is why They exempted the scientists and computer men and women from mandatory retirement at fifty and from the ten-year exile five years later.

Oh, They did have their value scale. Otherwise we would never have been allowed to go on living in this house. This was our reward for our "creativity," however archaic, however useless in current terms. It was also, let's face it, a convenience to them, for the honored groups of the self-sufficient left room in the planned communities for the those less fortunate (in Their terms). For I am quite sure that most of the old vastly preferred all the company they could get in their final years. Isolation would have killed them even sooner. For us, conversely, it proved our salvation, as did this house.

Jeff's family had owned it since the twenties, and when I married him we spent all our weekends and vacations here. So did the boys—later, of course.

I have called it, properly, ugly: all wood and shingle with a round tower with a conical roof at one end, and a deep, covered veranda all the way around it which keeps the lower rooms dark even on a blazing day. What's more, all of them except for the kitchen were paneled in dark wood. Until, that is, we managed to scrounge some paint and Barney led a work team to paint them all white.

It sits on a slight rise, surrounded by high wild privet, bayberry bushes, and long grass; and all you see from it is sky, fields, a few abandoned farmhouses, and the ocean, barely an eighth of a mile to the south. Or at least that is what you used to see when the fields were cultivated and the farm-houses inhabited. And before the storm you used to see a scatter of shacks on the dunes and rows of neat little ranch-type or A-frame houses on the formerly empty fields.

But Beryl fixed all that. The most vicious hurricane of that decade, she leveled all the jerry-built little vacation excrescences and junior executive "second homes," as they called them. The farmhouses nearer the sea were badly hurt, although—built at a time when workmanship was a clean word—they were susceptible to repair. But the sons of the farming families who had lived in them had sold their fields to the developers and left either for city jobs or warmer climates, and the times were then so turbulent, with the takeover, that few cared to spend the money for their repair.

So, because they were unsightly and unproductive, They burned them down.

As for our wooden monster, half the roof was blown off, the porch supports partly wrecked, and the windows—of course —blown in, or out. But Jeff and I clung to it like a spar in what was becoming the shipwreck of our lives and our world. In that last year before the exile we sunk every remaining penny we had in repairing the roof and propping up the main supports, and we ourselves cleared away the appalling debris and mopped up the mess. The old place looked worn and battered, but it stood.

■ Yesterday was Blind Day. It had become such a habit after a year that going about our daily tasks with masks closely fitted over our eyes was no longer an event or a challenge, even though we wanted to do it.

[51]

It all came out of a talk we had one night about the senses. We were afraid more than anything of losing not only our health but our faculties. It was partly in defiance of Them, but largely because we felt that our survival depended on a pattern of activities and disciplines followed at regular intervals.

It was also to prove something.

"You remember," Lev said, "that before we were put away there was a lot of talk about 'the enlargement of consciousness.'"

Barney groaned.

"Yeah," said Joey. "Multilevel perception. Everything going at once—sight, sound—Christ, what sound, it blasted you off your seat in those—what did They call them—electric circuses?"

"The theory was," said Lev, "that this meant increased awareness, that with all these new sources of communication one sense impact at a time was not enough."

"Shit," said Barney.

"Well my theory has always been," said Lev, "that if each of our senses—sight, hearing, touch, smell, taste—was developed to its utmost capacity we would then have attained not only total physical awareness, as in animals, but total spiritual development, as in man. Ideal man."

"Everything," pursued Lev, "atrophies without use."

"Including the sexual organs," said Joey.

"But of course," said Lev.

We also came to the conclusion that in depriving ourselves periodically of the use of our eyes or our ears or of one leg or hand, we would strengthen the remaining faculties to the extent that any possible affliction or decline in any of these areas would be compensated for by the heightened functioning of others.

So, after considerable wrangling and some grumbling, we

decided on a schedule of deprivations one day a week. Blindness, as I said, we achieved by nonslippable masks we made ourselves, deafness by earplugs, and the others by straps or slings devised by Barney that would immobilize an arm or leg. We couldn't figure out a way to deprive ourselves of taste that wouldn't also deprive us of food, which would be unbearable. We discussed touch at length, but the presence of two musicians, one painter-craftsman, the official typist (me), and a cook (Annie) made the sacrifice of both hands not only impractical but repugnant. We were damned if we would forfeit any of these pleasures even for one day.

On the other, reliance on one hand forced both Lev and Joey into technical exercises and improvisations which they would normally have neglected. The flute, of course, was out for Lev, but there was no limit to the fooling around both men could do on the piano, one hand each.

On One-leg Day, Barney just sat and had Annie bring him everything, but he thrived on Deaf Day because he didn't have to listen to what he called crap from the rest of us. Joey hated Deaf Day because nobody could hear what he said and he refused to shout. Lev, on the other hand, used it for reading scores, of which he had managed to salvage a trunkful and in which, he maintained, he found new things every time, even in orchestral and operatic music he knew by heart.

Annie carped continually at one-handed cooking (we alternated hands at regular intervals) but had to concede that it was possible, if irritating. I refused to type with one hand, but in time we found that we were becoming entirely ambidextrous, a source of satisfaction to each of us.

[53]

We pinned up a schedule of these deprivations on the kitchen bulletin board and, with rare exceptions, stuck to them.

But it must be admitted that the first months were shambles, particularly on Blind Day: everybody knocking into everything, cursing, stumbling, and bruising. It is incredible how far we have come since then.

For as time went on and we knew our way around, inside and outside, we became not only enormously proud of ourselves but began to hear and feel things we had never heard or felt before. We could identify the smallest sounds of insect or bird, the species of stone or shell or grass, the speed of winds, the quality of rain. Our sense of smell became acute, the soles of our feet (in summer we wore no shoes) had eyes.

Our skin told us the position of the sun, and the slightest variations of sound when we moved told us how near or far we were from each other or things. And for some reason, I don't know why, we spoke better when we were blind, perhaps because there were no distractions.

Lev was sure that he played better too, again, one supposed, because of the exclusion of all but sound and touch.

But the best thing blindness gave us was, astonishingly, love. And if anyone in this enlightened era still thinks, as the young usually do, that this is the exclusive province of youth, let them disabuse themselves. For we, the dispensable, found after the first year of hell here that not only couldn't we dispense with it but that physical intimacy itself was a natural element in our survival.

(I guess I should have expected it, but when I got back to this I found a trail of comments)

Tsk tsk! (*Joey*)

Speak for yourself. (*Lev*)

Please tell Joey to keep his hands to himself. (*Annie*)

How can I tell who I'm speaking to until I touch them? (*Joey*)

■ The first year here was hell for any number of reasons for each of us.

When the rest came to join me in this house I was still drained by my husband's death.

We had come to live at the house when They "retired" him at fifty. Jeff was an architect and city planner. His master plan for providing these necessities within the framework of political and financial realities was on the verge of being accepted at long last when the ax fell.

On top of this, the forced separation from our two sons, who—although one worked in Washington and the other lived in San Francisco with his family, used to visit us often—this loss hurt him as much as it hurt me.

Agonized, fearful, and powerless, it seemed, to stem the new tide or oppose it, we fled to this house after They finally gave us permission to live here rather than in a planned community of the "old."

From then on the life began to ooze out of Jeff. Without his work, without his colleagues, without external stimuli he sank into progressive depression. I had always thought that the male menopause was much more severe than the female transition, and now I saw what becomes of a man when he no longer feels himself one. Our sexual life had been gradually ebbing the last five years, but we both felt this to be natural (in spite of the manuals) and still took pleasure and comfort in each other's arms. We were great, close, friends; and that, we knew, was the best that a long marriage meant.

But now the shadow of impotence—the monstrous fear of it—was followed by its substance. He would lie still with his back toward me all night long, whether asleep or awake. And then he began to sleep in the next small room. Neither of us could bring ourselves to talk of it. Both of us knew.

I cannot speak for a man, but I know that next to not being spoken to there is nothing worse for a woman than not being used, or touched. Not in passion, for that can be spent, but in warmth. But a man who, it seems, must prove himself, is tortured by humiliation when he cannot. My own suspicion is that Jeff's humiliation was intensified by a society so sex oriented that nothing but spontaneous combustion counted in a vocabulary singularly free of tenderness. I suppose with diligent application to certain techniques (not, I may say, unknown to either of us) the spark might have been briefly rekindled. But neither of us were good at the clinical approach to what had always been instinctual, and his fear and shame grew such that he preferred to bury desire rather than not achieve its fruition.

After about a year of this alternating tension and sadness, I told Jeff I thought we should surround ourselves by giving shelter to certain friends who would otherwise be herded on reservations. The house was too big for two anyway, and I felt this was the only solution.

After long discussions—mostly on the difficulty of living with Barney—we finally decided on the five and immediately set about finding from the Central Agency where they were and how they could be transferred. This took months and was ultimately approved only because, as I have said, They made certain exceptions for the productive as against the unproductive old. Top marks for achievement, and all that.

It was in May of that first year before the others came that it happened. Next to Christmas, which he loathed, spring was a time of special depression for Jeff, and always had been.

This May he had withdrawn so much that he spoke very seldom, and then of impersonal matters. I knew he had not been feeling well—he complained of a strange heaviness in his legs and an ache in his chest—but he refused by entreaties that he go to the medical office in our district for an examination.

"Are you crazy, Kate?" he said. "Don't you know what that means?" And added, "Anyway, isn't their quarterly checkup due next month?"

Even in good health we dreaded this, lest they find the indications of a degenerative disease to which They offered only one solution.

It was a glorious day, with practically no wind. The sea from the bedroom window was placid, and when I saw a wedge of swans coming toward us from the pond I called Jeff and ran downstairs and out on the grass to look.

He seemed not to have heard me, so I watched alone as the great white birds with their necks far-stretched flew over against the transparent sky with a sound like wet wash flapping in the wind. They filled me with love and wonder, as the wild geese did with their high triangles and their distant gossip in the late cold light.

When the swans at last disappeared over the fields, I turned into the house again and called Jeff, for I was reluctant these days to leave him alone.

But he was not in the house, so I looked for his long thin figure on the road to the beach, but did not see it.

He had been gardening—his tin wheelbarrow was by one of the fresh-dug beds—for this was one of the few things now that gave him any joy and it seemed strange that he would interrupt what he was doing.

I looked behind the tall wild privet that had only just burst into small glossy leaf, and I looked in the shed behind the house, but he was not there.

Then I walked to the sea. It was the only other place he could be.

I hurried as I neared the beach and rounded the low dune. I looked to the right and saw nothing and I looked to the left and saw, far away, very small, the figure of a man near the edge of the water, facing it. He must have been at least a quarter of a mile away.

I started running and I kept on running on the hard wet sand. He was beginning very slowly to wade into the gentle surf and I ran faster and faster with my heart beginning to burst. By the time (spent with effort and anguish) I had reached where he had been, he was already far out and swimming steadily toward the horizon. I plunged into the icy waters calling and calling but when I came out of a low wave and looked for him he had gone down. Even if I could have reached where he had been I could not have saved him. I was already half paralyzed with cold and despair, and it was all I could do to swim to the shore and lie there shuddering in my sodden clothes.

I don't know why I didn't do what he did. It would have made much more sense. Day after day and night after night I wondered and flayed myself and ached for him and wondered again. What was there to live for now? Even the solace of our children and their children, and his mind, his face, his voice, his gestures reborn in them, was now denied.

And then the guilt: What did I do, what did I not do, that he could not bear to live? What grossness in me made me want to live? And for what?

I had long since known that men were the more vulnerable and women the more tenaciously rooted in life; but I never thought I would be proof of it. The fact is that I could not, would not, drown. I still cannot understand how Jeff, a powerful swimmer in his salty element, could deliberately swamp his lungs with water and go down. I could not; did not.

But day after day I walked the beach. And later in summer when the water warmed I would choose the days of roughest surf, plunge into roaring, towering water, dive through the glassy walls and out beyond, saying take me, suck me down and under, take me down.

But I was lying. I wanted to live. There was too much strength for waste, too much rage for resignation.

■ Last night, in bed, Joey asked me why I had written all this about Jeff.

"It's part of the story, isn't it?"

"Yes," said Joey, "but . . ."

"Too revealing? Too close to the bone?" He said he was merely surprised, because I had never written about intimacies before.

I said I hadn't because one didn't expose the living to hurt or humiliation.

He snorted. "What do you mean 'one'! *They* did!"

I conceded that They did and that I envied them.

"But why now?" he persisted. "To get it out of your system?"

No, I said. Just to write the truth, because what did it matter now and to whom?

He was quiet for a while, his arm behind my head.

"Poor bastard," he said.

■ The cutoff date was 1925. By that I mean that anyone born within the first quarter of the twentieth century was marked for segregation after They had come into power and when the new constitution was put into effect. Those over fifty, in short, were to be removed from contact with the young, including their own, and from the mainstream of life in self-contained communities and with a number of very definite restrictions as to the manner of life in general.

Granted Their outrageous premise, these seemed relatively liberal compared to the "final solution." We were permitted to live either in a community or in our own houses, provided that these houses were isolated from urban centers and concentrations of the young, and reasonably close to computerized service centers especially set up to provide the needs of the old, specifically food and medical attention for minor afflictions.

These communities were formerly middle-class suburbs from which, according to Them, most of the infection of resistance against change had come: the homes where the young had been brought up and against which they had finally and totally rebelled, thronging to the old and new cities and leaving their parents alone. As these older people died, their houses were preempted for the officially designated exiles and quarantined, as it were, from participation in the new society.

The nature of this quarantine was clearly spelled out. After two years of research and discussion, They had arrived at the conclusion that psychological, rather than physical, deprivation was the major agency of death. Of these nonphysical deprivations, they concluded, excommunication (or, if you prefer, absence of communication) was the most potent.

So those of us over fifty were cut off from any interchange with those under fifty, and of course that meant our children and grandchildren, and with the world at large.

Except for Agency communications we were provided with no mail service, in or out, no radio or television (nor, later, the far more refined instruments of communication), and no means of transportation except a sort of enlarged golf-cart, powered electrically and permitted only to groups of six, by which we could carry our provisions from the shopping centers to where we lived.

We assumed by now that there were no newspapers or magazines, since all news and information and entertainment was transmitted electronically. We were, however, allowed to take with us a limited number of books each and ten records, along with any record players we might singly, or corporately, possess.

The aging then had nothing to feed on except their memories, which they exchanged with each other until they no longer heard each other, and their usually pitifully limited inner resources. Most of them (and the young were quite right in this) had not really lived at all. Lived, that is, with physical and mental awareness and the experiences that derive from both.

A government agency—the A.A., or Age Administration—was set up to supply us with all our physical needs and the allowances (in scrip) to pay for them. This included the medical services I mentioned and any amount of sedatives—all free. They were really very kind to us, when you thought about it.

They were also quite right about letting us kill ourselves off. From what we could gather, the death rate in those earlier years, largely from oversedation, rose sharply even among presumably healthy people.

When any of us reached the age of sixty, we had to submit to a computer checkup at the Center. Those of us who were found to suffer from a mental or physical condition making us a burden to the community were painlessly disposed of. If we persisted in general health until the age of sixty-five, we were given a choice: self-disposal or compulsory liquidation.

This was really very liberal of Them, considering that every year of our useless lives was costing them that much more money and administration needed for the new exiles. They were more compassionate than They were given credit for.

If any who read this are amazed at this statement in the light of what must have seemed to all but Them a monstrous act of cruelty toward those whose only sin was age, I must say two things. One is that our first reaction was indeed compounded of outrage, shock, terror, despair, and confusion. We knew things would change but had no real conception of the scope of the change, nor of the extraordinary efficiency involved in it. The computer saw to that, as it saw to everything.

But the shock receded gradually and gave way to numbness and later to acceptance by the majority of us. The adaptability of the human being is, as you will see again in this chronicle, almost unique among living forms, and what begins as a gross abnormality can end as a familiar condition.

What begins . . .

■ Lily was one of the many reasons why our first year here was so painful and so difficult. For on top of the initial shock of exile and troubles of adjustment among six highly individual people who had never lived together in such unrelenting proximity before, Lily was the Great Divider.

There are some women who set up destructive vibrations the minute they enter a room. Sometimes beautiful, sometimes not, they are disrupters of harmony, rousing emotions of lust and envy among men and women that shatter whatever unity of mood had produced it.

Lily did just that. Joey and Jeff and I had watched it happen quite often at parties before the exile. She was not really beautiful in feature or structure, although she had fine skin and hair and walked in a rustle of fragrance. That she exuded sex from every pore was evident: a sense of the used and lubricated body matched the general invitation of her eyes and mouth.

Understandably the men clustered. Understandably the women—even attractive women—felt defeated and insecure where a moment before they had been confident and gay. Wives did not dare ask their husbands what they thought of her. They knew, even when their husbands gallantly murmured that she was "not my type."

But Lily, in a limitless field, was very selective. The semaphore may have winked "Come one, come all" but the thighs opened only for the rich or famous, especially if they were married. There was no challenge if they were not, although one of Lily's characteristics was a wide-eyed amazement, a profession of dismay at whatever mayhem she had so unwittingly wrought. Poor Lily, she would say with infinite charm: Why does this always happen to me?

It was inevitable then that it happened to Lev. And it must be admitted that, after the public furor about his divorce and remarriage died down, he looked ten years younger with the radiant Lily at his side. And even her enemies were forced to admiration for her when, only three years later, she followed Lev into his exile rather than remain in the world of youth to which she was entitled.

At first in this isolated house, she took enormous pains to please. She was a good listener, a gay and frivolous talker, and apparently as much in love with Lev as he was with her, so long, that is, as she did not talk about music. Lily was the kind of woman who has a box at the opera and subscriptions to orchestra concerts and knows nothing about music. It evoked pleasant sensations and allowed her mind to wander, and she would clap and shout "Bravo" at the close of a performance by a famous virtuoso. But that was about it, and Lev knew it. And when she once exclaimed breathily, after he played, "I'm mad about Mozart!" he looked at her with undisguised contempt and snapped, "I doubt if it would have been mutual!"

It was not Lily's fault that she was fifteen years younger than some of us, a reality we did not choose to be reminded of daily. Nor was it her fault that Joey became obsessed with her. It was inevitable. It would also prove disastrous.

During the first year, the lack of communication with the

outside world was very hard to bear, except for Barney, who had long since taken his leave of it. That meant, of course, that Annie too had turned her back on a society that had rejected her husband and in whose doings she had not the slightest interest.

But the rest of us felt like addicts in the first stages of withdrawal. The fingers itched for a knob to turn, the ears turned like radar fans to catch voices that never came; and the absence of newspapers or newsprint of any kind was— to Joey and me especially—a severe though comparatively short-lived deprivation. The awful truth of the matter was, as most of us had discovered in vacations in remote places in our earlier lives, that news ceased to matter; or, strangely, that returning to it, it had changed so little except for the death of friends or further evidence of some monumental human stupidity.

What hurt us most, though, was the denial of mail and telephone service to the "old." In this They were quite logical, of course, since it meant the complete and final break between our generation and that of our children and theirs, and that without this contact we might well prefer to die, pining away from love not bestowed or received; unable to comfort or counsel on the one hand or be regenerated by young minds and voices on the other. We ached to know of our children.

For the first year of exile; possibly for the second. But as time went on, we grew tougher, more ingrown, more—out of a kind of calm, defiant, rage—engrossed in our own survival. The splendid irony here was that, without the example and reminder of youth, we were less and less reminded of age. I am speaking again of us, here in this house, for many of the "old" we saw on our weekly provision trips to the

[65]

Center seemed to dimish, to shrivel steadily from their deprivations. I can only assume—and we talked of it often—that the reason for our comparative strength lay in the fact that four of us had led individual lives and performed individual functions apart from, or together with, our family relationships. Lev and Barney and Joey and I existed on other levels, in other worlds, and although human ties were—with varying degrees (for Lev and Joey seldom dominant)—important to us, they were not our only reason for living. If they had been, I could not have survived Jeff's death, nor any of us the cruel amputation of our young.

There was another, considerable, bonus in our lack of communication with the rest of our society. We were no longer able to measure ourselves by what others thought of us. Barney, of course, had solved his own particular problem long ago by never reading art reviews after the one that described his last—and lovely—show as "a skillful exhumation of dead values" and "an epitaph to the late and unlamented pigment past." But the rest of us continued to torture ourselves with the judgment of whatever individual, group, or institution held the current key to acceptance. Joey, even after years of public acclaim, winced at reviews that suggested that his "lyric sentimentality was out of step with present reality," and Lev used to explode at the frequent charge that he rejected the "new composition" simply because he did not understand it or the spirit that produced it.

As for me, I was increasingly tempted to give up writing altogether in a climate that held clarity obsolete, style suspect, and coherence the obverse of imagination. I tried once to write deliberate nonsense and was so uneasy that it might, under a pseudonym, be accepted as evidence of talent, that

I tore it up. I am now sorry I did, for it might have been honored by one of those very long, very learned articles characteristic of small intellectual reviews dedicated to difficult reading and the scratching of mutual backs.

But now we were blissfully free of these evaluations by those more clever, more perceptive, more attuned than we. We faced ourselves squarely, admitted our limitations, delighted in our talents, laughed at our presumptions, said, in short: to hell with them, we are as we are. This was not complaisance, but completion: the root of a healthy ego. Even Barney, so long without it, was beginning to regain it through carpentry and gardening and now, just lately, in the fashioning of things not for use but for visual delight.

■ After six months Lily could not stand her confinement with us any longer, and who could blame her? Not even Lev's infatuation and Joey's thralldom could make up to her for the lack of social life, of audience, of fresh conquest, which was her natural soil. Her tricks remained potent only in circulation and change, and she had no resources to compensate for what she must have thought the deadly continuity of deprivation.

Deadly too was the enmity between Lily and Phu, who— as I intimated earlier—shared an obsession with Lev that could be called mystic-erotic. Cat and man had a secret understanding that became an increasing aggravation to the woman. Phu in turn lost no opportunity in displaying his hate of Lily. He would sit on some surface above her head staring at her as he stared at Trilling, twitching his tail and moving his haunches sideways under him, and then, when she was momentarily unawares, would land on her shoulder or lap with a flying leap and sink his teeth into her wrist. Or he would dart out of the shadows and clutch her ankles with his paws, drawing blood and rage from the pretty woman.

Lev would laugh, swatting Phu lightly, with a gentle admonition, and Lily would blaze at him and Lev would laugh some more and say, "But you don't try to understand him, you think he's an animal!"

So one day when Lily went with Annie and me to the Center for provisions, she visited the medical office on the pretext of having Phu's scratches examined and attended to and was never seen again. She had, of course, complete freedom of movement assured by her all-purpose punch card; and she rejoined Their world.

There was nothing Lev could do about it. For several weeks he raged and wept and walked alone or stayed in his room, doing God knows what; for he could not play or even concentrate on scores.

At first we did our best to distract him, then decided he had to work it out himself. And then one day, when Joey was at the piano stumbling through a Chopin waltz, and we heard Lev shout: "Joey, Joey, not like that!" and then heard other fingers play with a clear difference, we knew he was on the road, away from Lily.

■ Much later, long after Lily had left, Joey spoke of her. "Whenever that cunt came into the room I got a hard on. At night when she and Lev went to bed in the room above I went out of my mind. I could imagine everything, I went nuts." He gave a short laugh. "Talk about Onan . . ."

[68]

You may wonder why I dwell on Lily since she was here so briefly and is not really a part of this story; and you may think it is because of hate. I think we did hate her—Barney and Annie and I, and even Joey, after he had finally had her and the atmosphere of the house became unbearable. But now I think we are grateful to Lily for having raised its temperature. After what had happened to us—our removal, or rejection by Them—we had become neutralized, unsensual. Not because of our years—that was, and is, a fallacy—but because They had tabled us as useless, without further function as minds or bodies. You become what others believe, as a wife no longer desired by a man becomes undesirable to herself, and then, in consequence, to others.

Lily brought back the fever. The blood stirred in us again, desire and curiosity and above all the need for close contact began to flower into a kind of playful intimacy wholly free from possessiveness. Call it an exercise of the vital forces, call it need, call it collective love, call it, simply, pleasure. It was all these. It was also part of the total awareness that They thought they had, and we knew we had at last acquired.

Do I hear from the outer void whispers of "Disgusting—those old people making love with each other!"?

Then remember that without the presence of the young there are no old. Ironically—and until Michael came—this was our strongest suit. It is the sight of the unlined skin that focuses, to its loss, on the lined. It is the sight of burnished hair that makes the grey sad. Without these comparisons we were merely ourselves: speaking, feeling, touching, loving in our differences as human beings, as men and women. We looked into each other's eyes and saw the same light, we opened to each other and gave what we had.

■ I have kept all this section about Lily from Lev, for obvious reasons, but Joey insisted on seeing it because "he didn't trust me to be fair."

After he read it, he conceded that it was a pretty accurate account considering that a woman wrote it.

"I wonder who's screwing her now!" he sang.

"Do you care?"

"No. I just hope that splendid internal equipment isn't being wasted. She could teach Them a thing or two."

I wondered if there was anything They *didn't* know by now since sex had already become an open book for five-year-olds.

"Then why," Joey asked, "why the hell do you get so coy about our arrangements here? This is supposed to be an honest report on what the old folks do when they're put away, isn't it?"

I said yes, but since They knew everything anyway there was no point in spelling it out. After all I wasn't doing this to titillate.

"Why not?" said Joey. "You mean there's nothing left to titillate?" Maybe not, I said, in a wide-open society. They would say, "So what?"

"I don't agree," said Joey. "For all we know, the new generation now may be reverting to Puritanism, and it'll do them a lot of good to get a few clinical facts on the libido as therapy for the old folks."

I said I didn't think I could bring myself to write it, not because of any Puritan ethic or an aversion to four-letter words, but because overuse had made them meaningless.

"You got *one* in!" said Joey. I said I used it because nothing else so accurately described Lily, and that in a choice between the clinical and the colloquial I preferred the latter.

Something apparently still bothered Joey. Keeping it out of context with Lily, he brought it up that night. It went something like this:

JOEY: Kate was saying that one reason we're so unconscious about our age is that there aren't any young around to measure against. Point is, doesn't that work the other way too?

LEV: You mean that with *us* around, They no longer feel like a special group?

BARNEY: A superior group, goddamnit. What in the name of Christ is so special, so important, about being a teen-ager? Or twenty? Or thirty? Who the hell decided that any age was automatically superior to any other?

K: Our parents thought theirs was superior. We thought so too. That's why we wanted to grow up, to be like them— the grownups. The last thing we wanted to be was fourteen or sixteen, except that it was on the way to being twenty.

ANNIE: We thought they knew more than we did.

LEV: And they did. Not all, of course, but the good ones. They learned through the sheer process of living.

K: It's different now. The young know things we were never taught, that we can't even learn now. They speak a language of their own which we don't understand. And They know this. It gives Them the whip hand.

LEV: Which They have used.

JOEY: Okay, okay, but They're growing older too. What happens when They turn forty and fifty? What happens then, when They get the taste of age?

[71]

LEV: They will revolt.

BARNEY: Then why the fucking hell didn't we? Why?
Nobody answered.

■ If I have given the impression that after the exit of Lily
we were a happy little group living a life, however circumscribed,
of pleasure limited only by self-imposed disciplines which were
more like games, let me remind you of two things.

One is that we were nearing the end. The cutoff date for
Barney and Annie and me was within this year, as I write, and
the following year for Lev and Joey, although they insisted they
would not wait. We would go together, voluntarily, before They
came. It was miracle enough that none of us had become ill
enough to qualify as a "public charge" at the last inspection,
although Barney, with his arthritis, barely squeaked through.
But our time was nearly up, and we never forgot it. In some ways
it now seemed more a relief than a fear, for there were limits to
our endurance and resources no matter how fortified by will and
invention.

Much worse was the feeling of each of us that at any
moment another kind of end would come. Rumors about war
had circulated again and again at the Center in earlier years:
now close, now not so close, now close. But lately we had
noticed a steady diminution of supplies, a steady reduction of
our allowances that could mean only that the country was
preparing for crisis and diverting more and more funds for
other than social purposes.

We began to confess to each other that every time we
walked on the beach or across the fields we drew that dreadful

shape on the far horizon; the incinerating mushroom with the bursting heart of fire.

You might say: Why should it matter to us now, this alternative death? It mattered to us because it was the end—of everything that mattered to anyone. Of love, of life, of Them.

And They, after all, included our own blood and flesh. We had long since learned not to grieve for what we could not have: our sons and daughters and their sons and daughters. And yet They were, in a sense, our only hope and the only reason for the Articles of Faith we planned to leave.

■ When I say that we had absolutely no communication with the outside world I am not being strictly accurate. Our biweekly visits to the Provision Center, our quarterly checkups at the medical computer clinic, became an exchange of rumor and surmise with the other exiles about what They were doing.

For these visits, of course, we used the vehicle They issued (and of which I have written) for this single purpose alone. Our early-model small electric car had a maximum speed of twenty-five miles an hour and a range dictated by the amount of batteries issued to us each month at the Center. These were sufficient to cover two round trips of about ten miles each, or, roughly, twenty miles a month. Early attempts to hoard batteries so that some of us could alternate visits to Their forbidden enclaves farther away were frustrated by the fact that each car was clearly numbered according to the "reservation" to which it belonged and easily spotted by the A.A. highway patrols and escorted back to its prescribed limits.

The only traffic we ever saw, for that matter, were these A.A. cars, A.A. trucks, a very few electric cars like ours, and an increasing number of military convoys with types of equipment we had never seen before.

One might suppose that this innocent excursion would supply a welcome change of scene, but it never failed to depress us. For one thing, we never thought of ourselves as "old" in our isolated group, but when we saw the other exiles the weight and lunacy of our condition pressed in on us. Besides which, the other "old" fell into two equally dismaying categories. There were those who were obviously waiting for death, having given up life. And there were those who were only too delighted to have their last years so comfortably patterned for them, including the prospect of "easeful death." These, an apparent majority, wanted none of the complications of the outside world; they seemed even relieved to be rid of their families and free to consider only themselves and their immediate physical wants.

What got all of us down was the Complier Counter with its full array of drugs, sedatives, and barbiturates free in any quantity without prescription. We all knew, of course, that after the age of sixty all those adjudged by a computer to be either infirm of body or mind or harboring a terminal disease would have only two alternatives: to take a lethal dose of compliers of their own volition or be relieved of life by an injection officially administered.

This was what the quarterly checkup would determine. And this is why the white panel trucks we passed on our provision visits never ceased to remind us of the rapid turnover, either way.

As for the healthy, the final cutoff was sixty-five, and the alternatives the same. Nothing any of us could say to ourselves

[74]

or to each other could let us forget it. Yet nothing reason dictated could stop us from dreaming of the last-minute reprieve, of a counter-revolution that would restore us to humanity even if the price were senility and slow and painful death.

■ Except for the clinic, the Center was staffed by exiles who took the scrip we were issued in exchange for the goods we bought, whether clothes or food or minor household appliances. For the first few years a surprisingly generous allotment of drugs, cigarettes, and liquor were free to the old.

This—such inexplicably tender mercy, we thought at first— was the supremely tender trap. For we were invited thereby to bring on our own destruction gradually as drunks or addicts without hope of the treatment we were accorded (until the age of sixty) for curable ailments. From what we had learned over the years from brief Center gossip, about a fourth of the exiles took this course, wrecking their constitutions by steadily increasing sedation, alcohol, or smoking. How many of the subsequent deaths resulted from these or from mercy killing by despairing or horrified mates we never knew. Or wanted to know.

■ During the first year or two of our separation we had, as I said, some communication with the other exiles at the Center. But supermarkets—and this was very much like the ones we were used to—hardly allow much contact. You load your cart, you apologize to someone whose cart bars the aisle to yours, you reach the check-out counter, and the checker, unless a smile of recognition lights her face, merely checks you out.

Once in a while the vaguely familiar face of another shopper would trigger a few words: "Aren't you . . . ? How nice to see you! . . . How are things going?" But what could you say when there was no news but the chronic state of isolation that we all shared? You could shrug, or shake your head, grumble about allotments, about cold or heat, wind or rain. But not even about ailments, that mutual bond of the old. With an Agency official always in earshot, who would confess infirmity? We could only see it in each other; and pretend that we did not.

But then, one day, the checker hastily thrust a small sheet in my hand together with the receipt. The look in her face urged caution, so instead of glancing at it I stuffed it into my shopping bag.

Lev had got one and so had Annie, and in the car going home we examined them. They were all alike: one sheet of paper, manuscript size and containing about five single-spaced Mimeographed paragraphs. It was obviously not an Agency handout.

"Very interesting," said Lev. "This is an underground press. There is news here—"

"From what source?" I asked. I was driving that day and couldn't look.

"Somebody," said Lev, "got hold of a radio, somehow."

Since this happened so long ago and since we didn't keep the leaflets after they stopped (were stopped from) coming, I can give only a general idea of what was in them.

The items were dated, as in a news bulletin, and concerned both domestic and foreign news. I do remember that some of them confirmed our worst suspicions.

The racial wars were still raging within the major cities, with casualties in the thousands on both sides and increasingly harsh police measures that boosted the death toll and filled the prisons to crisis proportions. All moves toward integration had halted, with both Negroes and whites, militants, liberals, and bigots, pushing for a black state, separate and autonomous. The only real argument, it seemed, was when and where.

Our forces, now widely deployed in "defensive" positions along the China-Burma borders, had engaged in repeated skirmishes with Chinese task forces. The death of Mao had caused no softening of China's attitude, which—after our bombing of their missile base—was hardly to be expected.

Famine and social and political disintegration had brought the poor nations of Africa, Asia, and Latin America to a state of anarchy ripe for communism or to the rout of moderates by military governments committed to repression and censorship.

As the United States efforts to cure or contain the increasing focal points of infection continued to grow, with the consequent drain of blood and money, we became progressively more feared and hated by the rest of the world.

In short, the news was not very different from what it had been before we left: critical and profoundly depressing. Even the good news that a cure for cancer had been found was, for us, academic.

These leaflets also contained a few personal items of a local nature. So and so had just joined the community, so and so had died. We did not even want to know these things. All we really wanted to know was news of our young. (I cannot bring myself to call them—Them.)

So what we first snatched with avidity we were soon just as glad to be without. It increased our sense of helpless unease, it reopened wounds and sharpened anxieties.

Perhaps, like all confined animals, we had grown to prefer our cage to the wilderness outside.

While we were free and of the world each of us had tried to contribute to it some joy or illumination, small or large. Now there was nothing left for us to do but exist with dignity.

Why am I writing this? I ask it all the time, for I still don't know who I'm talking to and how much you know of what went on. The trouble is, I'm getting more and more confused about the sequence of time and what happened when, and because of that it may bear no resemblance to what really was or what you know to be true.

The point is, are you They? Or, during these years, have you changed? If you have, why are we still here? Why haven't our sons and daughters rescued us?

Surely by now the results of this monstrous divorce between old and young must have reaped a bitter harvest. Or is it not only possible but beneficial to exist without a past, to live without inheritance?

And is it truly possible that the printed word, the book of paper and type, no longer exists? We find this almost the most difficult to believe. That, of course, is the reason for my writing: this stubborn faith in the *word,* in the immortality of letters.

It is the reason too why we have decided, in the last year of the lives of most of us here, to leave behind us—what did I call them, Articles of Faith?—if only as personal epitaphs on the dead, common, past. Common to us, of course. We could not possibly presume to speak for a whole generation, but we could speak for that part of it through which we had lived and worked with constant awareness during the convulsions of change in the first half of the twentieth century.

So, like our individual tasks in this house and our joint

pattern and duties to keep our bodies and minds from degeneration, we put aside one night a week for hammering out these
Articles, to be interspersed between the rest of this timeless (in
the literal, not value, sense!) account of our exile.

It is a painful labor to define what you believe, by what you
live, which values you still hold to be true, which have changed,
which abandoned during our own spans.

We kept drawing up lists: sex, art, ethics, morality, beauty,
evil, and so forth, and then throwing them out. We were embarrassed by the consciousness—the self-consciousness—of the
task, fearful of not making coherent sense. And always, that
question: For whom?

It was Joey who managed to prime the pump one day by
saying that we had to work up a head of steam first.

"Why don't we look at what They've presumably thrown
overboard and start from there?"

Everybody tossed in something. I can't remember who
shouted what. "Form!" "Tenderness!" "Order!" "Tranquility!"
"Grace!" "Responsibility!" "Guilt!" "Craftsmanship!" "Inno-
cence!"

The explosion made us laugh.

Then Lev said, "Yes . . . that's as good a way as any to
start. It's the cutoff of memory, of the past. It's why we're here,
isn't it—the end of associations?"

This particular day, since it was too cool yet to sit outdoors,
we were in the living room, and it occurs to me now that I
have taken it so for granted for so long that I have never
described it.

Lev's last remark brought me up short, for the room where
we spent so much of our time was packed full of associations. It
would have caused the contemptuous despair of any fashionable

[79]

decorator or aesthetic arbiter of the sixties, except for those who delighted in what they then called "camp." If any of you who read this remember what that meant, you will have to judge for yourself whether the term applies.

It was, for one thing, very cluttered. It wasn't when Jeff and I lived here. Although we never wanted to change its essential nature by making it what it was never built to be (very bare, very light—no moldings, no balustrades, and so forth), we had cleared out a lot of long-accrued family junk and hung only those few pictures or drawings that gave us active pleasure. The furniture was dog-and-child-worthy, meaning totally undistinguished, beat-up, but comfortable. We had covered most of it at one time with simple strong fabrics in clear colors, mostly red, yellow, and white, which were now faded and shabby. By's hairs and Phu's claws had not helped. The rugs were mostly hemp and fiber matting.

What cluttered it, of course, were the treasured possessions each of us had managed to bring with us and each had equal right to look at. I am not talking of books, for books never clutter. Now wedged in between or on top of all the combined reading of our own family, ranging from Austen to Auden and Chekhov to Nabokov, from architecture to physics to *The Wind in the Willows,* and dozens of forgotten novels along the way, nestled the stepchildren of this new family.

Grove's Dictionary, of course, for Lev; Joey's *Fanny Hill* (a reminder, he said, in case we forgot); Barney's *Notebooks of Da Vinci;* Annie's Red and Blue Fairy Books (her cookbooks were in the kitchen, of course), and something Lily had left behind on Beauty Diets.

There were lots more, of course. I doubt if we could have survived without a complete Shakespeare, the great Russian novelists of the nineteenth century, and good old Gibbon. Aside from these there were very few books left by now that we really wanted to read again, and fewer that were written after the Second World War. Offhand I think of Thornton Wilder's *Ides of March*, the poems of Frost and Roethke; and there must be more. But it was the toughest of all tests for a book (as well as a being) to survive this long in continuous and compulsory intimacy.

No, the clutter was on the walls and the tops of shelves and tables, window sills and any available ledge. Barney's sketches, Lev's family photographs (in silver frames) and his profile of Brahms at the piano, posters of Joey's shows, odd pieces of pewter and inherited silver, my shells, Barney's stones—all these things reminded me of a bowerbird's nest or, less lyrically, a junkshop. Twice a year one of us would threaten a complete clean-out, but when it came down to the objects to be removed, the outcries of their owners were so loud and grievous that nothing was done. As the house owner, however, I had managed to insist that the wall space around two paintings be left in peace. One was a Blakelock of dark trees and a moon, which Jeff's grandfather had acquired. The other was an Eakins portrait of a great-aunt of mine, which hung over the mantel.

The other few good things we had—a Matisse houri drawing, a Picasso etching, and one of Piranesi's magnificent prison series—had to fight the competition. And won.

Of the art of the sixties, color reproductions of some of its best-known painters were between book covers. I once came on Barney squatting on his haunches with the pages open to a furious pinkish whirl of whore's flesh, haunches, lips, and labia.

"Goddamn son of a bitch," muttered Barney. "What a thing to do to a woman!" He then riffled through the book until he came upon a design of heavy, rough black strokes, like crumbling girders, against a white background.

"Bow down before this great contemporary master!" he shouted. "He can only do one thing and that's it, and that's supposed to be enough!"

"Barney, why do you torture yourself? It's over, they're probably old hat now, forgotten . . ."

"Oh Christ, Kate, I keep asking what the hell I missed then, I keep trying to see what was great, and then I look and for the life of me I can't." He turned to another page—white, again, with three large black blobs and some falling dribbles. It had a title like "Death of Man" or "The Human Comedy."

"Fellow got five thousand clams for that," said Barney. "Look at the size of their signatures—I call 'em the 'signature of limitations.' They inflate nothing because they say nothing, it's the arrogance of poverty . . . their own arrogance, their own poverty. All these bastards did was scream, 'It's me, see, it's me!'"

I told him again to stop looking, that at least they were done by a human hand, that now he would be faced with the works of computers, wholly impersonal. I begged him to stop tearing himself apart for nothing. But he was sunk in gloom for the rest of the day.

To return to the room itself, we had come to love the mess we lived in. Not merely because we had no choice, but because these rooms and their associations nourished us.

"I had very rich friends," Lev said, "who had hired the finest of modern architects to design their house in Westchester. I went there sometimes for weekends, and I was overcome by the flawless purity of everything. Not one useless object, not one ashtray that was not perfect in design. Mostly white and black, with one small touch of color here and there. Only very modern art, mostly geometric, but some smears. Not a newspaper or a magazine ever visible, nothing every thrown on something, not a book lying open. It was utterly without content, without association. It had absolutely no human past."

"I could not live in such a place," said Lev. "However beautiful in an abstract way. I could not live without a sense of the past, without continuity."

"You really go for this God-awful mess?" asked Barney, sweeping his hand around.

"To which," said Lev, "you have liberally contributed!"

"It is not a mess," said Annie. "I like it. It's cozy."

"It's full of crap," said Barney, "but what's wrong with that? One of the best smells in the world is manure, and all you have to do to understand our secret love of crap is to watch Kate's face when that big animal of hers squats on his haunches."

"You are a child," said Lev, "a dirty little schoolboy."

"Look," said Joey, "I'm with Barney. Even the textbooks say it's one of the world's great satisfactions."

I report this kind of conversation because it is entirely typical. We ranged from the sacred to the profane with the utmost ease; I suppose because all of us had come to cherish the functions of body and mind as equal and inseparable. They were also far more fascinating than repellent.

This applied to our animals too. It was at first hard to explain to Joey because, city-street boy that he was, he had never lived with them. But in time even he recognized By's state of mind by his face. He conceded that the dog had a happy smile as opposed to the merely panting smile. That his

[83]

look was clearly sheepish when he missed a throw or a rabbit. That a bored yawn was different from a tired one. That the separate rhythms of tail-wag meant different things. That there were silly, excited, or angry barks. That his twitching dreams were very real. And that he loved me more than anybody else.

"Except me, of course," said Joey. "You know, when you start rubbing the back of his spine and he gets that lecherous look, I'm damn jealous!"

Phu's beauty, of course, was in continuous evidence except to Annie, who, as I have indicated, found him the incarnation of evil, the demon spirit. To the rest of us he was a joy to see, from the cream of his body and sable-tipped ears and nose to the incredible pale incandescent blue of his eyes, darkening as the black line of pupil expanded with shifting light and feeling. His leaps were miracles, his relaxations utter, his language inscrutable except to Lev, although in time we could distinguish the sound of anger from the sound of love, hunger for food from hunger for attention. I do not think any of us loved him except Lev. But he was part of the natural environment that we had come to cherish, along with the sea, the earth, the plants, the birds, the rabbits and voles and muskrats, as the greater reasons for our survival, the companions in exile.

So, on this particular night when we finally decided to make ourselves clear about the things that mattered to us, we were all in the room I have just described, after dinner. Lev in a worn but elegant garnet velvet smoking jacket with a foulard scarf tucked into the neck of his shirt; Annie in one of her several muumuu-type garments (this one a sort of dark blue burlap); Barney in his usual shapeless pants and one of the three old Breton's fisherman's blouses of faded canvas that never wore out; Joey in a raveling black turtle neck (which I was always darning) and corduroy pants; me in my tunic-and-slack uniform, this one yellow.

By was lying with his head on his paws just in front of the fire; Phu was draped over Lev's knees; Trilling in his cage and under a cover.

Once in a while a gust of wind would rattle a pane or whistle through a crack, but we lived with wind a great part of the time and heard only the rare silence when it did not blow.

And this, as well as I can reconstruct it, is what we talked about that night and called ARTICLE I:

BARNEY: Association is now the crime in art. Anything you paint, draw, carve, weld, cast, or hammer must not remind you of anything you have known, seen, remembered. . . . "Abstract" was the first word of the New Litany. Tell 'em what your precious dictionary calls it, Kate.

K: "Concerned with pure form and pattern, not representing forms of visible world . . ." Then it says that abstraction is "withdrawal."

BARNEY: Ha! That's it! You take away. You take away recognition, memory. You take away common inheritance.

LEV: I suppose the equivalent in music is to remove from it anything that might conceivably convey the sound of running brooks or folk songs . . . or the War of 1812 . . . anything, as you say, that might trigger recognition, that would distract from the pure . . . the abstract . . . pattern of sound.

K: But Lev . . . when I listen to you and Joey play . . . for that matter, when Jeff and I used to listen to Bach or Mozart records, they triggered off very distinct emotional associations . . . moods.

JOEY: Dirty romantic words.

K: I can't help it, I feel this enlargement, this sense of

[85]

tragedy or nobility or exaltation . . . it's abstract, I guess, but it doesn't take away, it gives.

LEV: I think we ought to leave music out of this for now. It has other elements, quite separate, that have to do with internal rhythms, with physiological reactions and so forth.

JOEY: Yes, I want to get back to those in song writing, but I agree, that's a separate—but associated!—story.

BARNEY: Look, I want to get back to this fucking word "abstract." Every goddamn day I pick up a stone or a piece of wood on the beach or a shell that's pure form. But it's not abstract because it's full of associations. It has meaning because an animal lived in it or ocean currents scoured it or salt and sun bleached it. The fact that you know these things *gives* it meaning. Now I'm not saying that if you paint these things that's art—although it's a hell of a lot nicer to look at than a soup can . . . and incidentally, if you're going to talk about representational art, those boys in the sixties turning out soup cans and car fenders and flags and comic strips were just as slavish and detestable as the Victorian pricks with their arrangements under glass and their painted china. There's nothing new about copying and scavenging, whether it's machine parts or dead rabbits, and nothing new about sticking 'em all together and calling 'em Art.

K: But surely, Barney, that's dead by now.

BARNEY: Maybe. It was dead when it started. But where did they go from there?

LEV: The last art opening I went to was gigantic pieces of machine-tooled metal or plastic. I forget what they called them, but they were certainly free of associations. You could look at them and feel absolutely nothing at all.

BARNEY: But that's it! That's what the bastards wanted!

Nothing! Negation! No responsibility of the artist to say anything! See what you want . . . feel what you like . . . Don't feel anything!

ANNIE: But Barney, you would not say that of Brancusi . . . of Arp . . . of Moore . . . they were abs—

BARNEY: Oh for Christ's sake, Annie, they had all the associations in the world . . . birds . . . eggs . . . heads . . . pelvises . . . haunches . . . hips . . . boulders . . . all the elemental shapes in rest or motion Purified, sure. Abstracted, not really abstract. And sensuous as hell. You had to *feel* as well as look. There were even a few sculptors working in the sixties that gave you that . . . they were craftsmen, and boy what a four-letter word *that* got to be!

K: How would you define craftsmanship, Barney?

BARNEY: Control of the material. Love of the material . . . time . . . effort.

LEV: You don't believe in the accident? The spontaneous. . . . what did they call it? . . . Happening?

BARNEY: My God, can't you people see this for what it was? What else is there for a piddling talent to do but abdicate will . . . control . . . choice? It's the easy way out!

Oh sure, there's a moment in everything you do when suddenly—wham, socko—something breaks free and you know it's right but you don't really know how it happened. But that's the product of mastery, not of accident.

K: I know what you mean. You slog away for days trying to find the right way to say something, and then—sometimes in the middle of the night—the words come. The right words.

JOEY: Hell, that happens all the time in music. But much more *after* you've written a hundred songs than before.

[87]

ANNIE: How *do* you start a song, Joey? I always wanted to know.

JOEY: Associations, natch! Simple things you hear people say . . . in bars . . . on buses. That is, if you're writing your own lyrics. Could be just two words . . . "alone again"—or "call me tonight" . . . anything. And then you think of a phrase . . . and it grows from there.

K: But it must be more than that.

JOEY: Sure it is. You gotta know what the human voice can do . . . how it breathes . . . what vowels are bad for a high C.

LEV: I don't wish to minimize Lev's very popular talents, but his is a very simplified form of what, say, any orchestral composer—any *good* composer—has to know about any instrument . . . and that *includes* the human voice.

K: Aren't we simply saying that you can't divorce art from humanity? And that humanity is the aggregate of human associations?

LEV: I would make it more precise, even. You cannot divorce any art from the physical roots of men and the natural world. But this is what has been happening and this is why nothing great has been composed . . . or painted . . . or written . . . in a long time.

ANNIE: How do we know?

JOEY: She has a point.

LEV: My God, aren't we living proof? How many times here haven't we said that there can't be a future without a past? And haven't They deliberately and voluntarily cut off the past and therefore the whole evolutionary process? Do you honestly think that electronic tape pieced together is the living organism of music?

[88]

JOEY: Man, it's full of associations! Sandpaper on wood . . . a police siren . . . traffic on the Long Island Expressway. . . . Aren't they the equivalent of your running brook and the War of 1812?

LEV: They are not, because my associations were the product of feeling. Yours are the process of doodling—of tricks and effects. Barney's "accident" again, or happenings. Maybe you can convey shock and novelty with pieces of tape . . . but tragedy? Ecstasy? Nostalgia?

JOEY: I often feel nostalgia for the Long Island Expressway. Common humanity trapped together.

LEV: It is this fragmentation again . . . the process of fission, not fusion, which was going on before we were . . . put away. Almost deliberate murder.

At this point Trilling began to sing in the next room. "There," said Lev, smiling, "is one answer." And then he went on:

LEV: It is not accident, you see, that that bird responds to fusion and not to fission. He recognizes the internal and external order of the universe, he responds to its rhythms, to the *associations* these rhythms set up in his own small body. That is why he is really only happy in the eighteenth century, in the supremely ordered clarity of Mozart and Vivaldi, in the magnificent *health* of their patterns of flight . . . or rest.

Lev suddenly bounded up, saying, "Wait, I have something I kept about this, it fits right in," and going upstairs.

Often Barney would shamble out when Lev took over, but he sat there and finally said: "Goddamn it, the Herr Direktor's got something there. There *are* patterns of flight and rest, they're timeless and organic because they're geared to the body— the eye—the hand. Those young pricks thought they could start from scratch—to hell with human needs, to hell with

[89]

associations, everything's new, got nothing to do with what went on before, long live the fucking new world!"

"The people who wrote folk music, popular music," said Joey, "know this. They know there's a beat and line that lifts the breath and the blood. Never mind the words, the good songs never die."

Lev came down with a very worn clipping in his hand, sat down, and put on his glasses.

LEV: Quite long ago . . . oh, I think it was in 1961, some doctors had a conference about something called the circadian rhythm. *Circa—diem*—do you understand? Around the day. My own doctor talked to me about it and I got very excited because it seemed to fit into so much about music that I had suspected for a very long time. As a matter of fact, I had long talks with a brilliant friend, an excellent musician who died some time ago, lucky fellow, who worked out a theory about the great compositions—the timeless classics of music—in which he related them—ha, associations again, you see—to the physiology of the human body. The pulse rate, the heart beat, the breathing, the walking or running. He gave actual examples at the piano—this was at a medical institute—of musical passages and phrases and themes—which corresponded—fantastically, I tell you—to these basic human rhythms.

And then, not much later, there was this very scientific medical conference—I really couldn't understand much of the report, it was so technical—but I cut out something one doctor said about this circadian rhythm, this sort of inner time clock that absolutely every living organism has, plant or animal, and he said, "All of us live within the pulse of night and day to which the rhythms of work and rest and eating and fasting are more or less routinely timed." He said rhythms of this kind are so familiar, so much a part of life itself, that we accept their significance as obvious. And he said, "I have wondered how many carefully planned experiments in the past have been confounded by failure to recognize the importance of circadian rhythms, how many experiments are being designed today, or will be designed tomorrow, innocently ignoring the same circadian influences."

JOEY: But surely, Lev, They're on to all that by now.

BARNEY: Well, They goddamn weren't when I was around. They were so crazy about all Their technological gadgetry, all those toys that They used instead of an eye or a hand.

ANNIE: Or a heart, Barney . . . They kept forgetting the heart.

K: But that's not wholly true, Barney, in fact it was the Hippies that revolted against all that, who wanted to feel—who came back to the body.

LEV: But what body, for heaven's sake? The dirty lazy body, sprawling around on dirty pads fumbling around with dirty girls to Raga music or psychedelic nonsense?

JOEY: Don't mind Lev, he's a roaring snob, aren't you, Lev? You really wish everybody was waltzing in Vienna to Johann Strauss.

LEV: I would vastly prefer it to jiggling adolescents in a howling black cave.

K: Don't let's start that all over again. It has nothing to do with association, and anyway, for all we know, They may have revived the mazurka.

(I said I'd edit this sort of comment out because it was not only outdated but unconstructive, but was howled down.)

"Hell no!" said Barney. "They're the victors, aren't they,

and we're the victims? We never had a chance when they took over, and now you're telling us we can't even say what we feel?"

We got into such a brawl that we decided to knock it off for a while and come back to it later, preferably with some coherent conclusion. If there could be one.

We were tired now, and it was late, nearly nine o'clock. Late for people who awoke at five or six and rose before seven: the pattern of age as well as diurnal rhythm.

In the future, in fact, these attempted formulations of belief usually took place in the afternoons, somewhere between three and six. In the mornings we were busy with our own chores and pursuits, and the evenings found us too weary to make any concerted effort of mind or body.

So we resumed ARTICLE I the following afternoon, outside. For once it was almost windless and the sun in a cloudless sky of American blue gave just enough warmth.

We carried wicker chairs and old cushions from the porch and put them on a grassy angle of lawn east of the house and sheltered from the north and west by the wild privet bushes that were now well over twelve feet high and very thick. Thick with small leaves, thick with birds, loud with birds.

Annie kept a birdbath always full of water well away from the house but in full view, and the feeder that Barney had made and nailed to the stump of a once-infected maple was daily replenished with scraps or, when we could buy them, wild-bird seed.

None of us except Annie had been interested in birds until they had become an intimate part of our daily experience. We were continually diverted by the way they bathed, the way they ate, the way the big coarse ones—starlings, grackles, robins—

bullied the little twitterers, the way they fed their young and signaled in song.

All talk would stop when one of the cardinals who lived in the privet would fly to feeder or bath. It is hard to describe what that pure and brilliant crimson flash does to one. It is a stab of joy, a sudden intake of ecstasy.

So, too, were the wild swans flying above, so white, with that incredible sound of whooshing feathers in air.

(NOTE: *I have just come back from washing some clothes to find these contributions from the unprincipled squatters I am forced to live with:*)

(*Lev*) I am *not* diverted by birds. They are noisy, quarrelsome, incontinent, and unmusical.

Phu is diverted by birds, but unable to express his natural instincts by a tyrannical majority who insist he be kept inside during these sessions. This is against all ecological principle.

(*Barney*) As to above, your bloody cat gets enough bloody birds on his off-hours.

To K: What, in Christ's name, is "American blue"?

(NOTE: *American blue is a blue you see only in America. English blue and French blue are entirely different, as any decent painter should know. I would say it was a hard-edged blue. We can argue later. Who's writing this thing anyhow?*)

We started today with the accepted premise that man as a species had reached the end of his evolution. No matter how long he might still exist on earth, his organism, the functions for which he was equipped, would remain the same. The fact that

[93]

his environment was altering radically, the fact that there were more and more tools to extend the range of these faculties, still did not alter the basic animal, man. By virtue (or limitation) of his blood, his bone, and his tissue, and because of this circadian clock, he would continue to respond to the same set of patterns and rhythms and impulses that had affected him during his entire span.

A man could fly three thousand miles in two hours, but his patterns of sleep, hunger, digestion, and so on, remained the same. The result was that these environmental changes, artificially induced, radically upset his internal rhythm—to his harm.

By the same token we felt that in the rush for new forms of expression, in the ignorance of, or refusal to recognize, these deep instinctual human patterns—rhythms—needs, They had begun a process of fragmentation extremely damaging to the human psyche.

We realized that this paralleled the increasing fragmentation of social life, of family life, of city life, but felt strongly that reflection of this, or even synthesis of this, was only a very limited part—the easiest—of the artist's function. His prime, his overriding, function was, so to speak, to pull the pieces together, to make whole and visible the internal—and eternal—pattern of life.

"Take the architecture of our cities," said Barney. "Who the hell wants to walk down canyons of glass, with no variety, no ornament, no history? A guy has nothing human to stick to, nothing to remember. He doesn't belong to anything."

"This is the whole marvel of the European cities," Lev said. "There are in all of them still enough old buildings on every street to remind you of where you came from—what you are."

Joey broke in, "You know, I walked a hell of a lot in New York but I kept making more and more detours to get away from those goddamned dead avenues and go on streets that still had old houses and crummy bars and crazy little shops—hell, even tenements. Anything was better than this faceless new stuff."

He said he once had to go and lecture on the musical theater at one of those huge multi-versities in the Middle West with acres of dormitories and study buildings all brand-new and shiny and dull and automated, and he said, "My God, if I had to study in a place like that I'd shoot myself!"

Again, we agreed that without history, without associations, without continuity, the three dreadful fates of deprivation—fragmentation, and alienation—denied man his essental humanity, his basic human needs.

And the arrogance, the coldness, of this denial was exactly what had alienated us from so much that had been painted, written, and composed in the decades preceding our forced withdrawal. It could shock, it could amuse, it could even at moments excite. But in the end, most of it diminished instead of enlarged, most of it provided no answer to these human hungers.

When we got to this point, Barney said something that I hope I can recall in full:

"You know," he said, "They were always talking about revolution this and revolution that, as if you could start one just like *that!*—from scratch, everything new, everything different, with no reference to the past. Phooey the past, to hell with it, like throwing out the garbage.

"But the key word, which They never used because it takes too damn long and They wanted everything *right now,* the key word is 'evolution'—which means a folding-out-from, a growing-from. So there's got to be a *from* to grow out of, and that *from* is the aggregate experience of man. It's a hell of a long line back, and although it may look like a cardiogram of peaks and wiggles, by God it's continuous . . . it's the *great* line!

"It's no accident," said Barney, "that the major changes in art have usually been brought about by middle-aged artists who had paid full homage to, who had mastered, the traditions of the past. They themselves had *evolved* as artists, as human beings, to the point where they said, 'Hey! I see this a new way, I think I see a new way to do this!' "

We suggested that these was again a matter of associations, that it took a long time to stockpile them out of the experience of living and looking and feeling.

Someone brought up the young geniuses like Mozart and Schubert and Keats, but we concluded that they were "freaks," born, somehow, with total experience. I think Lev used the word "possessed." But we agreed that, with such exceptions, most great talents got better as they grew older, and not weaker, whereas the early burst was apt to burn itself out before maturity.

We wrapped up the session by saying that a world without tradition, without inheritance, without the continuity which these implied, was—however affluent, however endowed with the fruits of technology—barbarian.

It was the word "barbarian," I think, that prodded us into examining the word "civilized." For if that was what we considered us to be, dying with the civilization that had nurtured us, we had to make it clear—if only to ourselves—just what that was. So that became ARTICLE II:

LEV: Civilization is a matter of form, or forms. If you are civilized, you accept forms which may have no meaning to you because they are part of a social machinery that makes life tolerable. If, on the other hand, you choose meaning without form—as the new barbarians have—you have anarchy—which means *Nothing*.

BARNEY: You can't have meaning without form, although Christ knows that's just what everybody was trying to do.

JOEY: Yes, but doesn't content dictate form? I mean, with me, the words of a song, the meaning of a song, determine the musical line.

LEV: Yes, but again, *within* certain musical idioms, *within* the limits of voice, or time—of audience attention. Of theatrical needs.

BARNEY: For God's sake, shut the musicians up, let's get back to human beings.

I suggested we stick with social forms, or, as Lev said "social machinery."

LEV: Look, this whole business of "respect for parents," for instance. By the time I was ten I had no respect for my father at all, although I loved my mother. My father was a charming, selfish Lothario who cared for nobody but himself, made my mother's life hell, and was not particularly ethical. But my sisters and I got up when he entered the room, said 'Yes Papa' and 'No Papa,' and learned to keep our thoughts to ourselves when he was around. We were brought up from infancy to respect not only parents but all those who were older than we, who had lived longer than we—*for that reason alone,* if for no other.

K: Yes, but They don't believe this any more because it's a "lie," it's not honest, it's exactly that kind of hypocrisy that They rebelled against.

LEV: Christ, since when has total honesty been bearable?

BARNEY: We've had a hell of a lot of it here!

ANNIE: Barney, Lev is right. I came from very poor people, peasants almost, but there was never any question about respecting them, even when we didn't. . . . It was hard with my mother, because she was a little crazy, I think, but—

BARNEY: You *think!* Christ, Annie, she was nuts!

K: Okay, but for decades we've all been told that this kind of artificiality, this dishonesty, if you will, warped the child for life, suppressed its natural instincts. I was made to feel guilty every time I tried to discipline my sons, to knock manners into them.

LEV: This is idiotic. Am I suppressed?

BARNEY: No, just warped.

LEV: Like most painters, you have no manners. I suppose you came from an emancipated household.

BARNEY: I was an orphan. I was brought up by my grandparents.

ANNIE: His grandfather beat him for every little thing. But they loved you, didn't they, Barney?

LEV: Well, this brings me back to my point. It is of course better to observe the forms of respect when the love and respect are real. But even when they are not, it is better that the forms remain, for without them there is no order and no peace.

I suggested that order and peace might be requisites of a civilized society, but that we had to be pretty careful about the kind of order and the kind of peace, because a police state or total stagnation might produce either.

JOEY: I agree. One of the worst things about middle-class suburbia as we saw it was "peace" and "order."

K: That's obviously not what we mean. Suburbia isn't the kind of organic order we're talking about, the natural order. It's imposed artificially, for business purposes—it's order for profit. It's sterile.

JOEY: It isn't peace either, it's conformity. It's a vacuum.

BARNEY: That nature abhors. Christ, all those lawns and those constipated bushes and cement driveways . . . no cover for any goddamn living creature, and everybody's cesspool fizzing with detergents and crap.

Annie rose and said she should go and start lunch, at which Joey remarked, "Talk about associations!" and even Barney laughed.

I said then that I could well understand the revolt of the young against those compulsive housewife-mothers who spent their whole time fussing over their lovely stemware and their bridge canapés and vinyl floors. I said that if I'd come from a home like that I'd probably have gone dirty in Haight-Ashbury too.

LEV: No you wouldn't, Kay. You have too much dignity.

JOEY: Ha! That's another dirty word! Let's get into that! We said, later . . . we hadn't finished the peace and order business yet.

BARNEY: I don't like that word "peace." It reminds me of those marble dames in robes with wreaths on their head.

Somebody started off on the Picasso dove, but I pulled them back and suggested "tranquility" or "serenity."

LEV: It is interesting that in all the arts—at least in the

sixties—this is the last thing anybody wanted—serenity. Shock—outrage—chaos—excitement—yes. But serenity—never.

JOEY: I think that's part of the go-go business. Action. If you stay still you're dead. You're dead if you don't move.

LEV: But surely movement can be serene. Good heavens, music is movement, and the great compositions have this tranquility—as *well* as passion and violence.

I wondered aloud if serenity wasn't the product of inner health, of balance, and that it was extremely hard to achieve in this kind of civilization.

BARNEY: But Christ, Kate, that's the point, this *isn't* a civilization, it's a violent, ugly mess! That's what They want, that's what the Barbarians want! No limits, no borders, no balance, no containment! Chaos is what they want, and by God they got it! Sick!

At this point Barney got up and stumped out of the room. There was a moment's silence.

JOEY: I think it's about time we defined who They are.

We turned to look at him as if he were mad.

JOEY: Oh I know, I know, but tell me something, Kate. Are your sons sick?

I said No, of course not—they had their problems but . . .

JOEY: Lev?

LEV: Alexandra? Eva? Don't be ridiculous. Difficult at times, but . . .

None of us looked at Annie: their retarded daughter had been institutionalized since she was seven.

JOEY: Well I can say categorically that neither of mine were "sick," as Barney called it. Jake went through the pot and pad and dirty feet business, but so far as I know he's still in archaeology, which is hardly a disturbed condition. Jennie married a rich guy and does good works. So who the hell are we talking about when we say barbarians? The new government? The computer kids? The underprivileged? Who?

ANNIE: Joey is right.

JOEY: If They're all barbarians, who are we speaking to, who are we defining for?

LEV: But surely we are speaking of people who are without discipline, without control, without manners, without sensibility.

JOEY: Too vague, too vague, you've got to be more specific.

Barney came in again and there was such a clamor of angry definitions that I finally shouted them down to suggest that they write their own lists of barbarians and give them to me to copy, because I couldn't possibly cope with this kind of gabble. They were diverted by this idea because tomorrow was Deaf Day and none of us had any desire to shout at each other.

Here are the Barbarian lists they made:

BARNEY'S (*printed in large crayon letters, gaudily embellished*)
    Editors of women's fashion magazines
    Most art critics
    Gum-chewers
    Generals
    Landlords
    Patriots
    Breeders
ANNIE'S
    People who do not love animals
    Men who rape
    Those who killed Barney
    Doctors who are specialists
    Salesladies who do not care
    Cats

JOEY'S

    Racists, black and white

    Fat cops, usually southern

    Charity audiences

    Agents, most directors, most cab drivers. Most drivers

    Those who produce and listen to greatly amplified sound

    Arms dealers. Gun-lovers

LEV'S

As I said yesterday, the mark of the barbarian—of whatever age—is a lack of self-discipline, self-control, manners, and respect for others. Barbarians are the by-products of distorted concepts of democracy and equality.

Democracy cannot survive without individual responsibility, and equality has never existed in the first place. Certain people *are* better than others and always will be, and it is only the barbarians who do not know this.

Our cities—as they were when we had to leave them—were full of barbarian hordes, honking their horns and littering their parks and making life intolerable for the gentle.

Barbarians are without dignity or grace, whether they are the fathers and mothers who drink too much, or the sons and daughters with dirty feet and no courtesies.

Barbarians come to concerts late and leave early.

Barbarians are without humility.

They are murderers of love, of beauty, of nature, of life.

Joey is looking over my shoulder. "Typical of Lev, isn't it, making a damn dissertation. *He* should talk about humility! Most arrogant son of a bitch I know."

I said maybe, but he was humble before music, and anyway

he had some points. In fact, by the time I'd read everybody's list, I didn't have much to add except this:

Barbarians are essentially people without a past or a future, living entirely for the gratification of their immediate desires. The barbarian is always an aggressor. He or she commits acts of aggression against language (obscenity), against sex (perversion, sadism, rape), against nature (despoilation, desecration), against love (nihilism), against art (anarchy), against life (war). The barbarian is a violator: the agent of violence.

Joey said, what about Barney, he was both violent and obscene, and I said that was a put-on. He was really the most vulnerable of men. And Joey said, well couldn't you say that about the barbarians—that they're lashing out because of inner hurt? That they're really sick?

So that got us back, next day, to what made a civilization sick—if that was really what we had become . . . or what we thought it had become before we were separated from it.

■ This morning Annie knocked at my door and came in and stood there. She apologized for disturbing me and asked whether I minded very much if she looked at what I had written about Barney.

I said of course not. It was the first time she had asked to see anything, and I wondered why.

"Any particular part, Annie? He's scattered all through here, naturally—as we all are."

"Some of the discussions, maybe," she said. "When he talks."

I asked her to sit down next to me and indicated several passages where Barney was more or less holding the floor. She read them in silence, shaking her head now and then.

"Tell me," I said, "if there's anything that doesn't sound like him. Sometimes it's hard to remember when everybody's cutting in . . ."

"Kate, it is—too true. Do you have to put in all those words?"

"The four-letter ones?"

She nodded. "I know it's the way he talks, he can't help it, but . . ."

I told her I'd thought about that myself, that it got repetitious, but that I tried one day leaving out the obscenity and it just wasn't Barney, it wasn't his cadence, it wasn't—well—him.

She sighed, hesitated, shrugged, and left.

This little interchange ultimately gave rise to a session on dirt: what was dirty and what was not. The cooperation was enthusiastic.

LEV: Our generation was unfortunate in more ways than one. We were born too late to enjoy the peace and stability of an elite society, and too early to cope with the most drastic changes ever to hit mankind. Then, we were the *pons asinorum* between the Puritan and the pornographer.

JOEY: Translation, anybody?

BARNEY: Christ, what a snob.

LEV: It's right up your . . . alley, Barney. *Pons asinorum* means bridge of asses.

K: I like the alliteration—P-P-P.

ANNIE: I still don't understand.

BARNEY: It's not for us peasants, Annie. In plain English the maestro is merely saying that we fell between two stools— which is what they called crap in our day.

LEV: Bravo, Barney! I didn't know painters were literate!

K: Wouldn't it make more sense if each of us said how we were brought up in that respect? I mean, in my case, for instance, my mother was extremely puritanical about bodily functions, sexual or otherwise, and would use euphemisms for everything . . . like Number One or Number Two.

Groans. I said I knew even then it was ludicrous, but that was middle-class gentility and there might even now be some Englishmen alive who said they had to "spend a penny."

BARNEY: For what, for Christ's sake?

JOEY: For Number One, dope.

K: No, for a pay toilet.

BARNEY: I see absolutely nothing wrong with crap or piss or fuck or balls or anything. Crap is exactly what it looks like, and piss is exactly what it sounds like, so what the fucking hell is wrong with that?

LEV: It is boring when used instead of language.

JOEY: What language? My God, Lev, the quotes lower classes unquote have used them since the first club fell on a caveman's toe and he said, "Shit!"

We agreed it was a deeply satisfying word, though perhaps not onomatopeic. Joey insisted it was, for birds: Trilling shit, whereas By crapped. Annie said Trilling did not shit, and Lev claimed that Phu "relieved" himself, and that anyway cats were far more civilized about their functions than other species.

There was intense argument about this, largely based on their language while mating, which all but Lev, naturally, found vulgar and repellent.

That brought us, of course, to the sexual words, at which point Annie rose and said she had something on the stove and left.

The four of us agreed that "cock" was a fine word and infinitely preferable to "penis," which was coldly clinical, but Lev and I had strong reservations about using the words "fuck" and "cunt" except in the most loving and private moments.

BARNEY: Okay, so what do you say? "Fornicate?" "Make love?" Too damn long, for one thing.

JOEY: What's wrong with "screw"?

Lev and I said it was merely feeble, whereas "fuck" and "cunt" had a basic inherent brutality, a contempt for the organ and the function which somehow degraded both. We put words like cocksucker and motherfucker in the same category and felt that their compulsive use not only in books and plays (accepted as works of high talent) but in the mouths of children were again the signs of barbarian decadence: the loss of those inhibitive values that were a part of civilization.

We wrangled over whether barbarism and decadence were compatible states, but agreed that the pendulum swing from what Barney called the "constipation of gentility" to the sanctioned diarrhea of obscenity had gone much too far. It struck me that these genital words, which ought to express intense pleasure and excitement if not love, had become the sort of shorthand of hostility and aggression.

Lev complimented me on the phrase but suggested something possibly worse: nihilism. The words had ceased to have any meaning.

LEV: They are the expressions of a profound, a terrible emptiness. It is what happens to a people who are so inundated with words that they cease to mean anything. As it is in so much of the music now, sound has become noise, signifying nothing. That is what They want: *Nothing,* as loud as possible.

JOEY: I don't agree, Lev. If anything brainwashed people into nothing, it was TV and radio, and God knows *They* didn't let any four-letter words on air. Hell, They called it a "family medium," and if anything represented the so-called middle-class-America values that the kids rebelled against, it was the monumental crap on TV.

K : The kids didn't make the commercials. I agree with Joey—the real dirt, the real nothing then wasn't dished out by the young but by the generation before them—the smart guys, the money people. That goes for the obscenity and pornography too. I don't think the majority of the young went for it.

LEV : What about those bearded groups who sang only four-letter words? The mass of our population was becoming more and more primitive, you had only to look at the streets of our cities and see the mixtures of the ghettos, the spawn of the unfit, those who should never have been born. *They* are the dirt mongers, the polluters!

JOEY : Harken to our great liberal. Ever heard of the melting pot, Maestro?

BARNEY : Damn it, let him say what he wants, you couldn't even whisper that sort of thing before we left without being called an anti-this and anti-that, but there are too goddamn many people in this world, and too goddamn many of them have to pull us down so they can pull themselves up! Maybe that's justice, maybe that's divine providence, but for Christ's sake, he doesn't have to like it, does he?

LEV : I simply do not believe in equality—spiritual, physical, racial, national, or musical. Joey is not as good a musician as I am, and it is not because his father was a second-hand furniture dealer and Joey never went to college, it is because Joey is Joey and I am I.

I said we weren't talking about equality, we were talking about dirt. I remembered when Sam went through a stage of appalling sloppiness at about fifteen and sixteen and got over it, but that Ben had already become a full-blown pot, pad, and barefoot swami at nineteen—dirty and loving. Why?

BARNEY: I'd be that too at that age. Only reason I wasn't when I was young was because I was brought up in a holy mess. Grandma was a lousy housekeeper . . . and when I grew up and wanted to be a painter, I found I couldn't work in a mess.

As Annie came back and sat down, she said, "You just *are* one."

LEV: But that's just it, Barney. The Hippies did not *believe* in work. It is a total fallacy that disorder and chaos are the natural companions of inspiration, of "freedom." From Bach to Stravinsky and back again, the best composers have lived lives of almost bourgeois regularity in terms of environment. I do not mean in human relationships—my God, look at Chopin, look at anyone you like—lechers—neurotics—pederasts—I mean the concrete details of their life were usually orderly, organized.

K: By adoring wives or servants . . .

ANNIE: Aren't they usually the same?

BARNEY: Ha! The old bag barks!

JOEY: What about somebody like Villon, for Christ's sake? Anyway we're not talking about geniuses, we're talking about our kids—or at least, the whole business of living in a physical mess.

K: I wonder if it wasn't mainly a revulsion against externals, against "appearances." Their parents were so obsessed with *things,* they were all bombarded day and night with brush-your-teeth-after-every-meal and Mom's shiny waxed floor, and "Whiter than White."

JOEY: And "You Have Bad Breath!"

K: Anyway, all that was a "big lie," a cover up of the real

human being. I suppose They thought it was more honest to be natural, not to care about these externals.

JOEY: To pick lint out of their navels: divinity through dirt.

BARNEY: They had something, by God. Here we spent billions of dollars to cover up man smell, woman smell, fuck smell—why? What the hell's wrong with smelling like a human being? Animals smell. You don't see that great black beast of Katie's slapping things under his armpits.

JOEY: He hasn't any—

LEV: Phu does *not* smell. My God, haven't you seen him at his toilette?

BARNEY: Only goddamn animal I know that can lick his own ass.

ANNIE: *Barney . . .*

K: But it's perfectly true, healthy animals keep themselves clean, dirt *isn't* natural to them, so dirt must be a sign of sickness in humans too.

JOEY: Kate, how the hell can you say that? Remember those all-American creeps who yelled "dirty Commies!" at anyone who marched in peace parades and had any hair? They took baths all right, but boy, were they dirty inside.

BARNEY: Same kind of guys who went to topless joints for tits in their highballs, but brother, peace was a four-letter word.

JOEY: P-E-A-C-E. P-I-E-C-E meant any dame except Mom.

K: I know all that. Just being clean is no sign of inner health, but the deliberate choice of dirt isn't either.

BARNEY: It depends on the *kind* of dirt. Sweat isn't dirt. Soil isn't dirt. Semen isn't dirt.

LEV: There is nothing dirty about good clean pornography.

Loud cheers from Barney and Joey, which Lev overrode with his podium voice. "Look. What has happened in the last twenty years is that manners of speech and behavior—and art too, really—have filtered up from the bottom to the top, instead of how it used to be for centuries—from the top to bottom. The violence, the brutality of the streets has invaded the drawing rooms and the so-called culture centers in the name of 'creativity' or 'truth.' The corrupted animal is king."

After the silence that followed this grandiose flourish I said that the king was dead: the whole concept of aristocracy, of an elite, had been dead for a long while.

JOEY: It's more than that. Look at us, for instance. The fact that we're civilized—or were brought up to think we were civilized—has doomed us. Good or bad, we're the last of a species. Hell, haven't you seen it in books and plays for years? The civilized were lousy copy, beneath contempt. The only people worth writing about were bums, brutes, junkies, whores—

I couldn't resist: "Or lovable neurotic Jewish families . . ."

JOEY: Whence all the good writers came, my girl!

LEV: The reason that they did not write about the well-born, the well-mannered—the few, that is, that remained—was that people like that lived by certain codes—certain disciplines of behavior and work—that at least controlled their animal nature. You might say it was the lid on the garbage pail.

JOEY: Now the cover's off and the stink is rare.

K: But it's not a stink to Them. In any case the "animal nature" is now considered the only reality. Whatever controls the stink and covers the pail is artificial—the deadly stamp of middle-class values—

JOEY: Whiter than White!

K: In all senses of the word.

■ We got back to it again last night: the question of what was dirty and then into what was evil.

I had been haunted by this all day and started off by quoting from one of my favorite Shakespeare sonnets:

"The expense of spirit in a waste of shame
     Is lust in action; and till action, lust
     Is perjurous, murderous, bloody, full of blame . . ."

I halted. It had been so long since I had known it all.

JOEY: I thought we'd agreed that lust was great—

LEV: Shut up! Let her go on!

I searched, faltered, then remembered this:

"Savage, extreme, rude, cruel . . . not to trust . . .
"Past reason hunted, and no sooner had, past reason hated . . ."

(Oh God, what happened to memory with age.) Then, suddenly, from that miraculous inerasable tape that we must have inside us, up welled a few more lines:

"On purpose laid to make the taker mad; mad in
     pursuit, and in possession so . . ." Wait a minute.
"Had, having, and in quest to have, extreme . . ."

JOEY: The fellow had talent.

LEV: I would say that it described every kind of physical excitement sought after for its own sake.

ANNIE: Not for love.

K: Not for love of someone else . . . for its own sake. For one's own sake.

JOEY: I would say he was talking about an itch—the gratification—is that it?—of an itch.

LEV: It is more than that. What was the first line, Kate? "The expense of spirit in a waste of shame"? I believe the important word there is "waste." Waste of self, laying waste of others.

I countered that I thought the business of this kind of lust being "bloody" and "savage" and "cruel" held the key. I said it was the sado-masochistic side of lust that made it, if you will shameful—evil. You inflicted pain on others and inevitably—in the end—on yourself.

JOEY: Hell no, Kate, I know people with strange habits who're happy as clams.

LEV: An astonishing phrase, I have always thought. How can clams be happy?

JOEY: There was something in the beginning of that poem that bothered me. Something in the first line or two.

I repeated again. "The expense of spirit in a waste of shame is lust in action; and till action, lust—" He cut in there.

JOEY: There, that's it. *Till* action, lust was bloody, cruel, and so forth and so forth. The guy's talking about fantasy here. He let's go everything in his mind before he actually does anything, and when it's actually done, he's disgusted with himself.

LEV: No, it depends on the nature of the fantasy. It depends on whether the fantasy is stronger than the reality. We all have fantasies—we need them, like dreams. But when the fantasy or the dream or the illusion becomes stronger than the reality, then we are in trouble.

JOEY: Yes, but that's not inflicting harm on others, it's merely harming yourself.

LEV: Which is a sin too. Kate here is always writing about my "vanity," well yes, if you wish to call it that. For me it is an enormous respect for the human body. I believe it is a sin not to care for it, just as I believe it is a sin to ruin a talent or a countryside—

JOEY: Or a woman?

There was an old flicker of animosity in the air, but Barney moved in. "Women," he said, "crave to be ruined."

ANNIE: Some women. (She looked at Barney.) Some men too.

K: All right then, Lev, could one say that fouling up one's body or one's mind or the bodies or minds of others are sins?

BARNEY: Let's leave sin out of this, I hate the goddamn word, it smells of ball-less men in black skirts and all that farting nonsense of church.

LEV: Perhaps the word "offense" offends you less, Barney?

JOEY: I'll buy "offense." I don't like "sin" either, a hell of a lot of sins were committed in the name of virtue, look at the Puritans. Anyway, you've got to admit, the kids did a lot to bury that crap . . . they brought the body back.

BARNEY: The hell they did! James Joyce and Henry Miller did! Renoir and Degas and Picasso and Maillol and fifty others brought back the glory of the flesh, kids have never started anything big, it's always the few gutsy people, and they're usually artists, who cut through the crap and show the way! Don't tell me the sexual revolution was made by these pre-nubile fur-bearing match sticks!

LEV: Bravo! You should have been a writer, shouldn't he, Kate?

K: It was all coming anyway. Money and sun had a lot to do with it. The rich lay on beaches and took off their clothes and then everybody started doing it.

JOEY: Doing what?

[113]

K : Hating clothes. The constriction of clothes. I hated bras and girdles and stockings and shoes and hats forty years ago and threw 'em away long before the fashions did.

LEV : It is more than that. It is an abandoning of all restrictions—or constrictions, as Kate called it—that comes with a totally free society—that is, a society without form or tradition. Casual manners and casual clothes go together. A man who wears a stiff collar must hold his head up. A man in a open shirt does not.

ANNIE : Lev is right. I always noticed the American tourists in Europe. Those men in the flowered shirts and those awful long shorts—they never stood up straight.

JOEY : They couldn't. Their Leicas were loading 'em down.

K : But those were the older generation. The young didn't look like that. Sam was quite a dandy when he was nineteen, sort of a Regency rake, and the girls he took out looked serene and romantic with their long hair. I simply can't believe that now in their thirties and forties they look like those tourists.

JOEY : Maybe not. Probably the cameras are lighter.

BARNEY : What the hell are we talking about?

ANNIE : I can't remember.

JOEY : We started talking about lust and got off the track.

K : No, we started with dirt—what was dirty.

LEV : It is very hard to keep *on* the track with this group. No discipline.

JOEY : That's right, Maestro. Why don't you conduct?

BARNEY : What the hell else do you think he's been doing?

K : I thought I was den mother, but how can anyone control this pack?

BARNEY : Don't try. We're the last living and breathing remnants of the tribe known as rugged individualists.

κ : Well, I wish I were a computer.

Joey leered at me, twisting an imaginary cap in his hand. "Please, lady, may I program you?"

I said that was the sweetest offer I'd had in a long time and took my disheveled notes to my room and dumped them on the desk.

They could wait.

■ I took a long walk today on the beach with By and came to a few decisions. One was that I could no longer attempt to follow the circuitous course of these talks we had and make any constructive sense out of them. They went too fast—and too far afield—for me to follow with any accuracy, and it was an increasing exhaustion to sort out from my notes and scrawls who said what and when. I could only—knowing them all so well—synthesize their comments, in the manner in which they spoke them (this came easy), and cut out the innumerable tendrils of digression or repetition which any group conversation inevitably sprouts.

This led to equally innumerable complaints from all except Annie (who spoke least) that I was leaving out this or that, distorting or confusing, etc., etc., to the conclusion that I would no longer permit them to kibitz on my script even if I had to sleep on it to preserve it inviolate. When I told this to Joey, he said it wouldn't work because the crackling would keep him awake.

The breath of time was blowing on us all. We knew we had not much left and that we could not waste it. If these pages have given the impression that we had forgotten our condition (and Theirs), it is a profoundly false one. We are continuously aware of death, for its probing fingers have touched each one of us.

With our next medical checkup imminent, Annie was worried sick about Barney's increasing hoarseness and the indisputable presence of arthritis. He complained continually of his back and shoulders while he gardened and had begun to transgress one of the survival rules pinned up in the kitchen: NEVER PUSH YOURSELF UP FROM YOUR CHAIR WITH YOUR ARMS. This was Lev's contribution to First Indication of Age, and it was proved to make sense.

The root of the hoarseness was, of course, something else: the presence of what was still (at least for us who were expendable) the enemy. If the medical computer established cancer, Barney's cutoff was very near.

Joey's eyes were bothering him. He kept saying that one eye was misting over and that he was sure it was cataract, but I said no, he just needed stronger glasses for score reading, and these could be issued at the Center.

Lev was becoming increasingly irritable for no apparent reason except the strains of propinquity, isolation, and void, which we had so far managed to contain, with continual effort. I suspected, though, that it had something to do with Lev's hearing. He was at his best on the Deaf days and at his worst on the Blind, when we depended so acutely on our ears and touch. He never spoke of this, of course, he would be too proud. But often I would see just the slightest inclination of his head toward a speaker, like the turning of a radar dish.

Annie seemed to have lost her appetite. She still cooked with sensitivity and zest, but she ate less and less, and for the first time since I had known her the fresh skin over her full flesh began to look like tissue paper, very finely crinkled.

As for myself, I continued to feel remarkably well but I could no longer bear to look at myself. My hair, my skin, my breasts, my legs, my feet told me what I had known in fact but denied in feeling. And even though Joey and I still slept side by side and made love probably more often than most at our age, the effort to sustain the fantasy and desire that had drawn us together was as mutually recognized as it was unspoken. In ordinary life I doubt whether Joey and I would ever have been lovers. I had always been strongly affected by beauty in men, and Joey had always shied away from what he called "brainy dames." But in this improbable nightmare context, simple need and amused affection impelled us toward each other into a protracted frolic—I can think of no better word—composed equally of laughter and love.

It was the loving companionship that remained, more like the tag end of a long good marriage than the late coupling of comparative strangers.

And besides, in the fog and the cold and the wind of so many ocean nights, we kept each other warm; and safe.

I doubt, from the little Annie told me, that she and Barney had even this solace. I knew that they slept in separate beds because when Barney was not snoring he had dreadful nightmares, and what saved her sanity was a small closet of a room opposite his that was used—sixty years ago?—by a maid. Their doors were always open so that she could go to him when he needed her, but he needed her more as nurse than as woman, and she had long known that without resentment. It was evident that she worshiped him, less perhaps for what he was now than for what he had been, although she would never have admitted it. Nothing could alter that; or her knowledge that he could have lived with no other woman but her.

As for Lev, he remained a mystery. Although Joey and I shared an often outrageous honesty, with no holds barred or subjects taboo, I could never bring myself to tell him what happened shortly after Lily left. He came to my room one night and without a word made love to me with an intensity, a brutality, and a virtuosity that would have enslaved me if I had not known, every second, that he was raping Lily and not me. I was, in the purest sense of the word, a cunt—without face or name—and a perversity normal to the promiscuous and now, for the first time, to me, made me exult in it.

Again and again that night he stiffened and swelled and came, and after he left—almost at dawn and still without speaking—I was bruised and overwhelmed. I could think of nothing else, want nothing else, for hours, for days, for weeks. But Lev never came again, never once spoke of it, nor even evaded me. It might never have happened at all.

If I had been a younger woman I suppose I would have felt cheated or abused or monstrously aggrieved. I might not have expected love, but at least a continuation of lust; and the abrupt cutoff would certainly have forced the anguished cry "What was wrong with me? Where did I fail?"

But not this time. I think I understood Lev. The amputation of Lily and his terrible need could make me anonymous for that one night in the wordless dark. But not in the daily presence of a woman he knew, respected, and, I believe, had fondness for. He was ashamed, and Lev could not afford to be ashamed. He could only expunge instead: me first, because he had never loved me; and Lily later, because he had. Thus the shame of his infatuation with her and of his use of me could—had to be—wiped out.

But what of his needs as a man? Joey and I talked often of this, wondering how any man of his highly conscious virility could endure the abstinence that this exile demanded of him.

"That cat," said Joey one day. "He may have trained it."

"Oh for God's sake, there are limits even to Phu."

"I don't think Phu's a cat. Phu changes into an oriental fag at night and does extraordinary subtle things." We discussed what these might be, and then agreed it would not be practical.

"Speaking of oriental," I said, "I think Lev has been through a sort of Yoga stage. He may just know the disciplines to control it."

Joey said, "I doubt it. Ever look at Indian carvings? 'All systems go' there all the time. Even the gods do it."

I suggested that the effort of teaching Joey to be a good musician were exhausting Lev. Joey said, what about *him,* and besides the one had nothing to do with the other. Sitting in an office all day shuffling paper or punching buttons might be de-balling, but not doing what you wanted to do. That was why creative people were so sexy, said Joey, making his leer face at me and panting like By.

Once he said, "Has it occurred to you that Lev may be much older than he looks?"

It had, but not after that night. So I just nodded; and continued to wonder.

■ It was dense fog the day the five of us went in our electric, super-golf-cart to the Checkup center. It made the excursion even more eerie than usual, and it had started off badly enough as it was.

Barney refused to go. He said to hell with it, let Them come and do it and get it over with, he wasn't going to stand in that fucking computer any more. Annie begged and tugged and wept, and Barney cursed and growled in his hoarse voice, and it took over half an hour of persuasion to get him in.

I think the argument that finally persuaded Barney was Lev saying that any irregularity on the part of any one of us might jeopardize all our lives—or what was left of them—and that while that might be all right with him, it was certainly not all right with the rest of us. We were not going to give Them that satisfaction.

So finally, in total silence, we moved through the fog, drifting in heavy and wet from the sea, lying low on the fields and roads, muffling sight and sound for the thirty minutes it took, but not the apprehension that choked our lungs and settled on our hearts.

To you who may read this, the computer checkup will be past history, too familiar for comment. But for us, even after how many visits, it never failed to remind us of the cataclysmic difference between our times and yours, of what you may have gained and what we profoundly missed.

Or to be specific, what we were already beginning to miss before you dispensed with us: direct personal care.

A few of us still had the family doctors who knew about people as well as bodies, who would pay housecalls when the urgency of our voices indicated the need, who could—just because they knew us so well—relate our ailments in many cases to conditions of mind and heart which affected this or that organ, lowered the resistance against this or that special infection.

But these mentors were fast disappearing in the wake of miraculous machines and the specialists who could program for them and read their language. These devices spared the doctors the tedium and time drain of listening to their patients, for the machines could tell them in five minutes or less what took the people fifteen.

Most of us began to dread the hospitals, which had not yet made the transition between human and mechanical care. The expense of the former was monstrous, and yet the money drained from us brought us neither solicitude nor compassion. What nurses there were had no time. They performed their functions in haste and—with rare exceptions—indifference.

Once in a while—long ago—Jeff and I had amused ourselves by looking at television serials about doctors and hospitals. The doctors were handsome young gods or wise old kindly men, the nurses smiling and pretty and tender, the wards gleaming and bright. It was grotesque in a country where public service was still light-years behind private enterprise.

Or maybe you have changed that by now? Have somehow managed to use the machine to free men—doctor and patient— for more and not less contact? For more and not less compassion? For more and not less human dignity?

If you have, we are not now the recipients. We go into this cubicle that looks like the inside of a space capsule, with panels of lights and buttons, and strange prosthetic devices that form a hollow man or woman. We are told by a recorded voice to step inside them, to breathe or cough or flex or relax as the devices contract or expand to fit us. And through the incredible ganglia of wires that extend from them (like a telephone circuit I once saw in a city exchange) go the impulses of heart, veins, blood, pulse, the temperature of skin and eyeballs, the image of lung, uterus, aorta, kidney—everything. The voice even tells us to "void" (that is still the word) into the small receptacle between our legs. (Barney hated that more than anything.

[121]

"Void, my ass," he growled. "How the hell can I piss for a record?")

But Lev and Joey claimed that the slight pressure of the foam-rubber-lined tube that held their cocks was more pleasurable than not, and they wished it took longer. Joey said, "Now I know why cows didn't balk at mechanical milkers."

As for women, the device had contractable cups for breasts—and if we had not known that it must be for the detection of tumors, Annie and I confessed to each other that the mechanical palpatation was not unpleasant.

But this was gallows humor, for each time the experience left us demeaned, degraded, and deeply fearful. What messages of deterioration, of degeneration, were sent for decoding through the wire cat's cradle? What decisions made by the strangers who evaluated them?

Why wait for their decisions? In the endless night thoughts we had, in the endless discussion we held about whether to make our own decisions, to take the compliers before we were ordered to, before the mandatory cutoff date, we wondered why we chose to live on Their terms rather than die on ours.

Each of us admitted to fear of pain, none of us to fear of death.

If pain became intolerable we had the means to end it. Since death was inevitable, what difference did a year or more make?

Did we hope or believe that there would be a drastic change, a social and political upheaval that would bring us back into common life again, end our exile?

It was certainly possible; but did we really want it? Yes and no. Our often intense, even agonized, desire to see our own young, our flesh and blood, after all these years was shadowed by almost equal fears.

Would the gap now be unbridgeable even with them? Would the mark of the exile, the alien, inexorably separate us from this new society? Would the adjustment to this new life—if that were even possible—be preferable to the balance we had so arduously achieved in isolation?

Balance. Had we indeed achieved it? Or was it the wrong word? Could it be the beginning of some sort of revelation? I think we all felt that we were on the verge of it, that if we could just—just—if we just had time to attain this condition of —enlargement of consciousness—wan't that what they were always talking about when the drug thing started, years ago— if we just had time. . . .

Then what? On attainment die? Or somehow share it? Why else would I be writing this weird tale?

"Maybe," said Joey one night, "we ought to call it the Book of Revelations."

"Isn't that a little presumptuous?" said Lev.

"Since when," said Barney, "haven't we been presuming? What do you do when you don't know a goddamn thing?"

"We only know what we have learned," said Annie.

I said that if she meant what we had learned out of our own lives, our own truth, it didn't count. It hadn't counted for a long while. You have to have college degrees, you had to have graduate degrees. At the magazine we wouldn't even interview any applicant without them. In the world of today we would be jobless illiterates.

"Kindly exclude me," said Lev. "You do not graduate from a gymnasium [he pronounced it 'ghim-*nah*-sium'] and the Polytechnik an illiterate."

Lev, of course, never ceased to extol the European education over ours, and in the sense that he could speak five languages fluently and had been acquainted since childhood with the history and culture of their countries, he had a point. Joey had had two years at Columbia before he bummed around Europe for a third, I had never been to college, Annie had not even graduated from high school, and Barney left—or was thrown out of —a small New England college after his first year.

Lev wondered how Barney could have acquired such a wide vocabulary without a university education.

"I picked it up at college," said Barney. "I was pure before."

"Bunch of dropouts," said Joey. "We should have been very popular with the kids."

"What was the phrase that cultist nut used?" said Joey. "Tune in—turn on—drop out?"

"Instant revelation," said Lev. "You chew something, you swallow something, and presto—the glorious universe is suddenly manifest and you are one with humanity."

"You stick a flower in your ass," said Barney.

"What I could never understand," said Joey, "is why they needed that. What the hell was so boring with life that they had to cop out of it? I'm turned on all the time."

That's how we got into the Book of Revelations. I told them to stop talking, to shut up, and to make a list of things that turned them on and to give it to me tomorrow. I also gave them strict injunctions not to be frivolous or facetious. It wouldn't do just to say fornicating or drinking, you had to be specific and serious. I also maintained that pleasures were not enough: it had to be something that lifted you to a higher plane of feeling, of consciousness.

Lev was delighted. It meant no interruptions in the full

measure of his stately prose, but Barney said what the hell did I think he was, a f——g writer? and Annie said she had never been able to express what she thought, and Joey groaned that he didn't have time, he had to practice his Ravel, and they were all so tiresome that I got up and left.

We started talking about it again later.

"Look," said Joey, "this isn't going to work if everybody looks at what everybody else puts down. I don't trust you bastards around here."

"My dear fellow," said Lev, "we are not all American students cheating at exams. Are we, Phu?" He held the cat out facing him and Phu made a negative sound.

I asked them what I was supposed to do: type them blindfold?

"You don't have to type them till they're all handed in," Joey said. "After they've read them."

We went even further. We asked Barney to make a sort of page-sized ballot box with a slit on top into which we could slip our notes and which wouldn't be dismantled until all the entries were in.

The box was kept on the mantel in the living room in full view. Any overlapping or repetition of ideas that emerged could then not be plagiarism but the spiritual propinquity that this common exile and common fate had brought about.

■ The Night of Revelations was quite an affair. Ceremoniously we brought the ballot box down from the mantel and then each one read his piece out loud.

We were all very touched by Annie's statement. Lev walked over and kissed her gravely, and Barney gave her a fierce bear hug and whacked her fanny.

Lev, as you see, was long and rather didactic, and the rest

of us tried to ignore Barney's shameless hamming: eyes rolling, sighing heavily, belching often. Of all this Lev was fortunately oblivious; in love, as usual, with the sound of his own voice.

I got the worst kidding for being long-winded and sentimental, although Lev defended me when I quoted him, and Annie shed a tear over "Western Wind" and Whitman on Lincoln.

I said I had a perfect right to take that much space because all I'd been doing before was reporting their interminable talk and emerging from these pages a cross between a den mother and a woman warden. Joey said he could add another description, but as that was in the nature of a revelation, he wouldn't.

We accused Joey of being appallingly mundane, but conceded that some of his comments were enjoyable and made sense. Lev said he could see no possible relationship between a headwaiter and revelation, let alone a vicuña coat.

The rest of us turned on Lev not only for his pomposity, with which we were all too familiar, but for assuming that we knew all that music.

It didn't take much urging (it never does with musicians) to get him to the piano to play some of his "revelatory" choices for us. Unfortunately he sang along with them in his horrible conductor's voice, but his passion for the music was impressive and encompassing.

Barney quite properly stated his terms of revelation in images. He passed around about ten drawings—some of them among his most dynamic—of a variety of things and juxtapositions. Quite aside from their quality, I couldn't help thinking: thank God for something I don't have to type.

Anyway, Barney leaned over our shoulders grinning foolishly as we admired each sketch.

But the best part of the evening grew out of a complaint that Joey didn't say which songs "sent" him (including his own) and that he owed us some examples.

Again, his arm needed no twisting. He sat down at the old grand and after a moment's silence started playing—and singing —twenty or thirty songs from the great musicals of the thirties through the fifties. Too many to set down here, but I remember us singing with him (a terrible chorus except for Annie) everything from "My Bill" to "Got the Horse Right Here" to songs from *Finian's Rainbow* and *My Fair Lady* and *Carousel* and *South Pacific* and of course, Gershwin. Lots of Gershwin.

It was a wonderful night, and if it is indeed in the nature of revelation to erase time—and with it, knowledge of death—then those songs were part of what we all meant.

The euphoria extended through the night. I don't think I had ever been so fond of Joey as I was then, as we lay together and I held that ugly face in my hands and his arms held me and I felt those tufts of hair on his chest and shoulders (the simian patches I had never liked in a man before!) and I told him how good he was and he told me the same, and in the darkness we were of no age; no age at all.

I thought of Lev alone in his room, and Annie in hers listening in pain to Barney's difficult breathing, and I blessed incredible fortune that we had each other. Perhaps we should have blest Them instead.

■ The euphoria didn't carry over into the morning. When I went to my desk to start lining up all the "offerings" I had left there before going to bed, no sketches were among them; or anywhere visible.

Later a red-eyed Annie told me why. Barney got up in the middle of the night and came downstairs. She followed him as he fished out his drawings and against her begging protestations tore them up and tossed them into the still-red embers of the fire.

"He was in an awful state," she said. "All those terrible words, and how he couldn't draw any more, he was finished. But why? Why? They were really good, weren't they, Katy?"

So all I can put down of what "turned him on" is my memory. Of an interior spiral of a conch shell . . . of a swan in flight . . . of the intricate patterns of twigs against the sky. I remember the buttocks of a horse right next to the buttocks of a woman—equally copious—and another association between a sort of muscular trunk of a tree (sycamore maybe?) and a man's twisted torso. Then he did one of the lips of a cowrie next to something very much like it that Joey pounced on with relish.

(Joey *would* walk in at this point. He says he did not pounce and that it was a vagina, anybody could see that.)

"And you missed that gorgeous boob," he added. "A real swinger!" I swung at *him* then and he retreated.

Lev reminded me later not to forget the one of the mysterious smiling mouth on a Cambodian head.

Oh yes, and a sort of a headstone in the shape of a cock, with a large wreath spelling B slung around it.

B for Barney.

This is what the rest of us put in the box:

ANNIE

Funerals of great men. Presidents, like Roosevelt or Kennedy. His brother or Dr. King. The march and the drums with people crying. And the horse with those things backward.

Very young animals, like little deer, who are helpless. The rabbit who trembles. The smallest bird—when the heart beats in the hand.

When the mother licks the young. Or a human mother with child at her breast. Particularly some Madonnas, I forget by who.

Hot sun on grapes or tomatoes. Not just the smell. How beautiful are God's gifts. It is a miracle, every time.

When I read of Christ or Abraham Lincoln. The pure heart.

When a man is tender with a woman. This is the greatest paradise.

The sky at night. To think of others there in the dark, on other stars. How the soul climbs to them.

(*I am sorry this is so short. I know there are more.*)

LEV

Strictly speaking, of course, revelation is supposed to be divine disclosure, or knowledge disclosed by some supernatural source. Since "divine" is perhaps not a suitable word for this Godless group, I prefer to use the word "supernatural" in the sense of what is not natural—what is not familiar, what is beyond the normal state of being to which we are accustomed. For revealing means something that we have not seen before.

It can happen, for instance, at the moment when one loves a woman. You have seen the woman before, you think you know her, but suddenly she is revealed to you as a new being, she undergoes a transfiguration through the supernatural agency, you might say, of love. You are lifted to a higher state of feeling where even one small hair on the back of her neck, or the touch of one finger, can bring ecstasy that is beyond the physical although it is of a physical, a "natural," nature. Thus you could say that when Barney draws a shell or a stone, he sees more than the shell or stone: he sees a divine order, a universal truth which lies at the essence of life.

This is what I see, what I feel, in certain combinations of sound which are at once suprahuman and also go to the heart of human truth. As we have said here often, these are closely geared to physiological, to natural, man—to his heart and blood, which in turn are linked closely to the mind and psyche. It is the essence of musical genius that these certain combinations of sound, which are abstract, still are able to speak directly to the nature of man, or rather to that nature of which he is often unaware. He is lifted to higher states of feeling and emotion in which he experiences a communion with the universe, a limitless largeness of spirit which the daily concerns of his life usually crush and extinguish.

(Note from K: What you see here I had to copy later from pages and pages of Lev's handwriting. I told Joey I felt more and more like a pool typist, especially as Lev never apologized for the lordly length of his comments or thanked me for transcribing them.

Joey had the nerve to pass this on to him, but Lev, it seemed, looked both imperious and innocent and said, "What else has she got to do?"

Irrefutable!)

L E V : I am not speaking here of the sentimental music that makes stupid women cry, or the military music that makes stupid men cry—these are popular tricks which anyone can learn. I am not even speaking of the best folk music, which of course can stir genuine emotion—feelings of pleasure and joy and well-being, even of sadness and loss, which can be also pleasurable. As for the tribal chants through which most of our young people searched for revelation in those days before we were parted from them, I can only say that the stupefaction of the mind through noise and physical ritual is the mark of primitive peoples not ready for knowledge. Without a highly trained consciousness, the unconscious cannot operate. Without a highly trained body, no Nijinsky or Nureyev could have leaped into other than physical dimensions.

My revelations are not confined to music: I can reach supernatural states of communion and ecstasy through a perfect glass of wine or the pink of a glacier in the evening light. But since music has been—and is—my life, it is natural that I speak of revelation in its terms.

I remember an essay that Felix Weingartner, one of the greatest conductors, wrote about conducting. He was speaking of Wagner and the Dresden orchestra. Beyond the essential need of technical "correctness," he said, Wagner looked for the "unifying thread, the psychological line, the revelation" (he used that word) which suddenly, magically, transforms a more or less indefinite sound picture into a superbly formed "heart-moving vision." Weingartner said that this magic made people ask themselves how is it that this work, which they thought they knew, should suddenly have become quite another thing. He said that then the "unprejudiced mind" joyfully confesses that "Yes, this is what it must really be!"

Now the young may sneer—they used to, certainly—at words like "heart-moving" or "noble" or even "joyful," there has—for so long been none of these qualities in the new compositions,

[131]

written out of a sick brain or a feeble spirit for "effect," or shock, out of contempt for simple humanity. I have conducted works of such complex monotony that it was all I could do to stir my men to any interest beyond their duty. They derived no pleasure from this tonal diarrhea because none was communicated by the composer.

Until the composers of music, I insist, are able again to "move the heart," to attain, by whatever physical or technical means they use, this transfiguration of the spirit, this profound sense of revelation in the listener, music will continue to be merely sound—a penetration of the ear—as art will be merely a penetration of the eye . . . physical manifestations of varying intensities incapable of enlarging the nature of man because it is not in tune with the nature of the universe.

If this nature—this universal truth—did not exist, its interpreters—a Bach, a Mozart, a Beethoven, a Leonardo, an Einstein—would never have existed.

It is difficult to talk of revelation in words, it is even more difficult to talk of musical revelation precisely because music is the most abstract of arts and therefore the most universal.

If anyone reads this—the child of the present cut off from our common past—he may say "What is this man talking about? What exactly does he think produces this 'revelation,' this 'enlargement?' What—and pardon the expression that must by now be entirely obsolete—what 'turns him on'?"

So, out of the prodigious literature of music (and for the benefit of my musically illiterate companions in exile) here are a few of the many, many passages in which the ultimate compassion, the ultimate nobility and transfiguration of which man is capable are made manifest in sound.

Although I know them by heart, from thousands of readings and performances, I cannot tell you the reason for this. It is "supernatural"—the product of forces beyond our knowledge but not beyond our recognition:

Of Bach there is such a wealth (how does one single out specific passages in the *B Minor Mass* and the *St. Matthew Passion?*) that I will merely suggest the *Partita in E major for Solo Violin,* the *Double Violin Concerto in D minor,* especially the slow movement, and the *Goldberg Variations.* The immense purity and passion of Bach is matched only, of course, by Mozart.

As for Wolfgang Amadeus, *Don Giovanni* first, perhaps. But again, too much to choose. *Concerto for Piano and Orchestra, K. 467? Symphony in E flat major, K. 543? Quintet in G minor? Quartet in G minor?*

For Beethoven, perhaps the second movement in the *Concerto for Piano and Orchestra,* Opus 58. The *Concerto for Violin and Orchestra,* Opus 61. The *Quartets in F minor* and *F major,* Opuses 95, 135; the *Sonatas,* Opuses 109, 110, 111.

Brahms' *Symphony in E minor,* of course, Opus 98; the *Concerto for Piano,* Opus 15, especially the second movement. *Concerto for Violin and Cello in A.*

I would certainly choose Gluck's *Orfeo* and Monteverdi's madrigals, especially *Lasciatemi Morire* and *Ecco Mormora L'Onde;* Schumann's *Dichterliebe,* especially "Ich Will Meine Seele Tauchen"—and probably the *Kreisleriana.*

The *Chopin Piano Concerto,* Opus 11.

Richard Strauss' *Four Last Songs,* especially the third and fourth.

Mahler—*Kindertotenlieder, Das Lied von der Erde.*

Really, there could be no end to this. No matter what I put down there would be fifty others. People would say, what, no Wagner, no Ravel, no Stravinsky, no Rachmaninoff, no Dvořák, no Tchaikovsky, no Moussorgsky, no Prokofiev? Of course. Glorious passages.

(Thank God there are no other musicians around. We would kill each other.)

Besides, this is a ridiculous exercise.

On rereading this, I am fully aware that anyone could compile a similar list from hundreds of other choices. Some may complain that most of these passages are so familiar, so well known, as to have become hackneyed. They would not think so if they conducted or performed them. The fine performer, in fact, is renewed each time he plays or sings them; it is only the routine professional to whom repetition becomes formula.

There is a clear analogy here too. If a man or woman truly love each other, they bring to each sexual experience a renewal of passion, they approach each other with a fresh sense of discovery. I will freely admit that this is rare, but so is musical genius.

In either case, the physical performance is only part of it. It can be technically perfect and yet empty of meaning. To be lifted to that other plane of being, other factors must exist and they are of a mystical nature. Again, part of an elemental, suprahuman pattern, only dimly seen most of the time (and often never by the damned, superfluous, millions of this earth), but now, in fusion, suddenly and supremely clear.

There is pain in this as well as joy, for there is no beauty without loss. Perhaps it is the tragic sense of man, or perhaps I should say the marriage of triumph and tragedy, that is essential to revelation.

Christ was right. You cannot find yourself without giving yourself. You cannot begin to live until you accept death. *Tod und Verklärung.*

JOEY

(Note to Warden K: Since there is censorship in this concentration camp (no f-k-ng, the lady says, no dr-nk-g), and a w-t c-nt is beyond my powers of description anyway, the list of things that turn me on will be short, if not sweet.)

The moment when a song jells and you know it. Even with your lousy voice, you know it's there, you've got it, it's off the ground. When the words and music come out natural as breathing, only with that extra catch, that beat that hits your guts.

After the hundredth performance of the show and some chick or male lead sings it for the hundreth time and the crowd goes wild. That applause, and the look in their faces, and Christ, I love the world.

Success. See above. God love the world when it loves you, headwaiters and all. It's a lot of balls about success being an empty thing. Maybe it is when it comes too easy, I wouldn't know about that. Out of several thousand songs and lyrics over thirty years maybe fifty get remembered, you work for it. If you still know when you write crap, you're safe.

[135]

When you hear music somebody else writes and you know they're better than you and still you're not jealous. You listen to the best of Jerry Kern or Dick Rodgers or Lenny Bernstein and you want to cry, it's so great.

This sounds crappy, but happiness turns me on. I mean, this is such a crud of a life, everybody you know's got terrible troubles, every goddamn human being's alone when you come down to it, so when you can make them happy even for five minutes or five bars, you feel you're worth something.

At a certain stage you couldn't care less if some half-assed critic says, "Your latest score is rich in rhythmic and melodic invention," but when some cabbie recognizes you and says, "You know, my old lady cries every time she hears 'Don't leave Me,'" I choke up too.

A vicuña coat.

Watching your daughter turn into a woman.

Lying in a deck chair on an ocean liner (do they have them any more?) and not thinking of a goddamn thing.

The first drink of the day. This is the one that makes you love people. You may say that this hasn't got anything to do with revelation, but there's been a lot of talk around here about a sense of "common humanity" and "being one with the universe," and boy if that's revelation, the first drink does it.

Thinking of my mother and father. Thanking them. I hope they get the message. I hope they never knew what a bastard I've been. But at least I know it.

Sleeping like spoons with you. (Either way around.)

General thoughts: About this thing of the kids turning on with drugs and such. I still think it's a cop-out. Okay, it's a tough world and this civilization stinks, but when a bunch of us castoffs can get turned on without swallowing or smoking, we must have something they haven't got. They know more, but could be they know the wrong things?

K

I am in love with so many things it's hard to know where to begin. It can be as small as the mole on By's right cheek and as large as a hurricane wind, but how measure revelation since it grows from the immeasurable root of love?

I love the sea: it is my resurrection and my life, the fluid in which I was born, the element which sustains. I give myself to it. It lifts and pummels and threatens and caresses, it makes me whole. I am in awe of its ferocity, grateful for its calm, amused by its perversity.

To be inland is a deprivation, as if, as a child, to be kept from a mother.

I am awed by a handful of sand, by the knowledge that each grain is a rock, a crystal, a boulder, a carapace. I enlarge them in my mind.

The shapes of shells catch my breath, even fragments indicate perfection. The sight of porpoises leaping is a leap of joy. The inside curl of a wave is miraculous.

So are the small birds pecking at the shoreline and the tern in a vertical dive and a wedge of duck winging so fast, and the stretched black necks of cormorants.

An ocean and beach in fog may be mystery but it has the stillness of truth. You wait, and the truth has to come.

The range is too great. The wind in wheat fields making spiral patterns and I think of my fingers in a man's hair or the rough cowlicks on By's back.

Thunderstorms and the terrible blanching light and cracking blows.

Rain on the roof, always a benediction.

I suppose I am as in love with the natural world as I am with man and animal. The revelation lies in the closeness.

My earliest revelations were through poetry and music. They came from poems of transparent purity and simplicity, and always those that sang.

I can put down here only those poems which I have remembered since I was eleven or twelve and can never forget. They will seem hackneyed to the intellectual ear: too familiar, too romantic, too simple. But then they were not addressed to the intellectual ear; they were sung in the wind to anyone open to them. (And they are as clear, as precise, as controlled as they are emotional. The divorce of mind and feeling was not yet sanctioned when they were written; and when my generation was young.)

> Oh Western wind, when wilt thou blow
> That the small rain down can rain?
> Christ, that my love were in my arms
> And I in my bed again!

> *Mère des souvenirs, maîtresse des maîtresses,*
> *O toi, tous mes plaisirs! O toi, tous mes devoirs!*
> *Tu te rappeleras la beauté des caresses,*
> *La douceur du foyer et le charme des soirs,*
> *Mère des souvenirs, maîtresse des maîtresses!*

I wish I were where Helen lies;
Night and day on me she cries;
O that I were where Helen lies
On fair Kirconnell lea!

Go and catch a falling star,
    Get with child a mandrake root,
Tell me where all past years are,
    Or who cleft the Devil's foot;
Teach me to hear mermaids singing,
    Or to keep off envy's stinging,
        And find
        What wind
Serves to advance an honest mind.

Tiger! Tiger! burning bright
In the forests of the night,
What immortal hand or eye
Could frame thy fearful symmetry?

When lilacs last in the dooryard bloom'd,
And the great star early droop'd in the western
    sky in the night,
I mourn'd, and yet shall mourn with ever-returning spring.

Oh how shall I warble myself for the dead one there
    I loved?
And how shall I deck my song for the large sweet
    soul that has gone?
And what shall my perfume be for the grave of
    him I love?
                *(Note to self: if this were not of
                Lincoln's death, would it still
                move me so?)*

Beauty crowds me till I die,
Beauty, mercy have on me!
But if I expire today
Let it be in sight of thee.

> *Les sanglots longs*
> *Des violons*
> *De l'automne*
> *Blessent mon coeur*
> *D'une langeur*
> *Monotone*
>
> *Tout suffocant*
> *Et blême, quand*
> *Sonne l'heure,*
> *Je me souviens*
> *Des jours anciens*
> *Et je pleure;*
>
> *Et je m'en vais*
> *Au vent mauvais*
> *Qui m'emporte*
> *Deçà, delà,*
> *Pareil à la*
> *Feuille morte.*

Now cracks a noble heart. Good night, sweet prince,
And flights of angels sing thee to thy rest!

What is it? Why these? Looking at them, so random over
the centuries, I try again to explain to myself what it is they—
and so many others—have in common that so touches, moves—
yes—enlarges me?

They are all cries of longing—for what is unattainable, for what is lost, for what is noble. They are full of love and death and they are fiercely alive.

And they sing. It is not just a matter of rhyme and meter, it is the ebb and fall of breath, the beat of the human pulse, what, as Lev and Joey have said, is the internal physiological rhythm of man which the artist *must* recognize, respect, and speak to.

Those young men and women with their guitars and their songs of love and rebellion knew this. I wonder if they are still singing, for the best of them found the beat: not just the primitive beat of the loins, but the cadence of longing and compassion that marks civilized man. I don't know if Lev agrees with me, but I always felt that these new troubadors were far closer to the great line of music than the self-conscious avant-gardists who fiddled with sounds for sound's sake.

Maybe what I'm trying to say is that revelation and universality are of the same stuff, and that this universality is not only one of space but of time.

In revelation you feel not only for your children but for all children, not only for your life but for all life, and any bomb that falls on anybody tears a scream from your throat. Place, or kind, anywhere on this globe ceases to matter.

In revelation, you feel time past as time alive. In the ruins of the temple of Poseidon in Sicily, the sea wind sweeping the long grass between the columns, you feel the presence of gods. From a ruined castle on a Hebridean promontory, down the steep cliffs to the cold sea and the spear-headed slip made for a Viking prow, and you see these men tie up and land. In a deep French gorge you hear the horn of Roland.

As for time not yet come, few of us are blessed—or cursed—

with this revelation, but of those few most of the diviners are artists whose imagination encompasses both reaches of time. Very often they are failures in their age, because the public is as brutal to those ahead of it as to those behind it. Fear of change makes cowards of people, and they reject the true prophet.

I know that before we were put away there had burgeoned a technology of the future, men and computers already busy anticipating the next ten, twenty, fifty, hundred years. But supposition supported by evidence is not divination: it is a conscious exercise of the mind, the "educated guess."

Revelation is the marriage of knowing and feeling. And where the one begins and the other leaves off, who shall say? Any of us?

■ This morning Annie, who is always the first to get up, came downstairs and found Trilling feet up in his cage.

I found her sitting next to it with her head in her hands: a boulder of grief. I looked at the small yellow thing on the floor of the cage with his claws contracted, his limp neck sideways, and his eyes filmed, and the enormity of it for this woman left me without words. I knelt down by her and put my arms around her and then she reached for me and started shaking. There was no sound, but the tears ran down from her cheeks and onto my shoulder.

There was nothing we could say of this death in the family. It was incredible enough that the bird had lived this long, but there was no solace for her in that. Lev started to say so as kindly as he could, considering his normally unconcealed irritation with it, then stopped halfway and said, "I am truly sorry."

Barney said nothing. He knew what had happened as soon as he looked at his wife. He went straight to the cage and lifted it off its stand and walked out beyond his vegetable garden to a small corner of earth between two wild privet and set it down while he dug a small hole.

Joey and I stood at a distance. Two old people with their dead pet, I thought. What would They make of this grotesque senility? What better proof to them of the useless life, its end—like the bird's—long overdue?

Barney started to open the cage door and reach in, but Annie, with an unnatural brusqueness, pushed aside his arms and took the small body out herself with extreme care.

She brought it up to her cheek and her lips moved as if she were speaking to it, and this was too much for us. We turned away and walked back to the house, in pain for them and sorrow for us all. It was our first casualty, and its size made no difference.

The day itself was a pall. It was extremely hot and humid, with dead air in which the tired August leaves hung without moving. The sky was without color: not cloud, not fog, but a neutral shroud through which a whitened sun shone intermittently, a baleful disk.

Joey and Lev tried to concentrate on a Mozart sonata, but after a quarter of an hour gave it up. Joey said the place where the cage had been got on their nerves, that Lev was an insufferable martinet, and they both knew the day was jinxed. We all were weighted down, blaming it on the weather.

It had indeed that ominous prestorm stillness, the unnatural suspension before uncontained force.

We spoke of hurricanes, and Barney threw himself almost savagely into the job of battening down the house and preparing for the worst. Joey and I admitted to each other a certain hope for it. What better, what more free and elemental end; without the agony of choice. Dylan knew it; not to go softly into the night, but to rage, rage against the dying of the light.

But the worst did not come. It was a bad storm, with winds that must have reached gale force, bending the trees half over and driving the heavy rain almost horizontally against our old shingles and window panes. We spent much of the night mopping up the water from the leaks, and much of the morning clearing the grounds of broken branches; and the seething roar of surf filled our ears.

Later, Joey and I wanted to have a look at the beach to see what the storm and high water had done to it.

The sky was still gray, with scudding shreds of clouds, the wind warm and wet. As we neared the beach we could see, above the tops of the coarse dune grasses, the furious spume.

The surf was immense, the roaring waves crowding each other, overlapping and colliding as they tumbled in, and the wind threw their collisions high into the air, hissing and booming as they tossed and fell.

By bounded ahead of us on the scoured sand, garlanded by heavy shiny dark brown scrolls of kelp but otherwise empty except for some sodden planks and one upturned tree stump bristling with roots.

Suddenly By stopped. And suddenly, the way the eye immediately turns to a movement of something that should not be where it is, I saw a dark knob tumbling in the surf. I was sure, with deep unease, that it was a head, and for one insane instant I thought of Jeff.

"Joey," I pointed.

"I know. Wood?"

"I don't think so."

"Nobody'd be crazy enough to swim in this surf. Those waves are murderous."

We both hurried forward, By bounding ahead.

For a split second we saw only streaming hair on what seemed like the head of a man. Then it disappeared under the roaring foam, bobbed up for another instant, and was sucked under by a new and towering breaker just as Joey made a move toward it. By started into the water but I called him back, and he stood at the edge, shivering and crying in his nose.

Then we both ran backward as the hissing turbulence raced toward us, with its human freight rolling over and over, and finally beached as the water withdrew.

We rushed to the naked body and together pulled it up as far as we could out of reach of the sea and looked at it. Lying on his stomach with his face turned away from us, his arms crooked upward in a pitch-fork U, was a youth. In spite of the firmness of his flesh we were sure he was dead. We were so sure that when one of his hands curled downward into the sand and the muscle of the forearm twitched, we were shocked and stupidly frightened. By leaped backward, whimpering.

"My God," said Joey.

We bent over as one and gently turned him over on his back. His head fell to one side, his eyelids fluttered, and he breathed with a shudder.

I had never done it before but it seemed the only thing to do. I straddled him with my knees and covered his mouth with mine and breathed into it while I moved one arm up and down and motioned to Joey to move the other.

I remember thinking long ago that I would never be able to

[145]

do this, to touch the mouth of a strange and possibly dying man with my mouth, but after the first feel of the cold wet lips ("I kiss your mouth, Jochanaan . . . there is a bitter taste on your lips!") aversion fled, and when I felt the warm air coming from them into mine a wild elation filled me instead. I lifted up my head to watch him breathe, more regularly now, and let go of his arm.

"Do you think he's all right now?" said Joey, letting the other arm fall.

"I think so. But he's cold. God knows how long he's been in the water." Joey was already pulling his shirt off his furry shoulders and chest, but instead of trying to put it on this apparition I thought it would make more sense to use it as a towel to dry him and get his circulation going.

"You rub his legs while I work on the top," I said.

Joey of course made some crack about reversing the order, and then shut up when the young man opened his eyes, gave a very deep long breath, and the faintest of smiles.

"You okay?" said Joey.

The young man merely continued to look at us, gravely now, and then covered his crotch with his hands. We assumed that he was too exhausted to speak.

Slowly he raised himself to a sitting position and reached out for the shirt, which I gave him. He put it over his lap and sat there, breathing.

We were, we later agreed, awed by his beauty. Biblical was the first word that came to me, but not at all in the calendar-Christ way, even though his black hair, crusted with sand and salt, came down below his jaw, and he had a short beard. And even though there was a John-the-Baptist gauntness in the architecture of his sun-darkened body and face, his mouth was the full and fleshy mouth of youth.

"Do you feel all right?" we said, and "What happened to you?" and "Where did you come from?" and "You must be cold," and "You must be starved," but he answered to nothing.

Before long, he stood, tall and very thin, and tied Joey's shirt around his hips, the sleeves knotted over his cock. And when we said, "Come with us, you must eat, we must help you some way," he came with us.

For a time we thought he could not speak, in shock from whatever had happened to him. But after that time we knew he could tell us nothing because he was dumb. And because he was young, we adopted him, whatever the consequences.

■ We called him Michael because he looked like the archangel. We had absolutely no idea where he came from but thought, after much discussion, that he might have escaped in a small boat from some school for afflicted children, possibly from some island, and had capsized in the storm.

I use the word "afflicted" not only because he was dumb but because he could apparently neither read nor write and seemed to have, in spite of his magnificent face and body, the mind of a child.

We blessed the isolation of the house because no one had seen him come and we took great pains to see that no one would see him here. Keeping him inside was of course impossible, and so was hindrance of his walks outdoors.

Except for the first few weeks, when we never left him unaccompanied and seldom went far from the house. One day Joey said, "Look—Mike is about the same size as Lev. If Lev grew a beard like Mike's you couldn't tell them apart from a distance. They just couldn't go out together, that's all."

It took some time to persuade Lev to cover any part of his face, but the combination of his fascination with the boy and our repeated assurance that he would be twice as handsome with a beard finally bore fruit—or rather, hair.

I told him also that a beard was an erotic asset, and that cinched it.

By the time Lev's beard had matched Michael's in shape if not in color, we learned as much as we could of someone who could tell us nothing. And the more we learned, the more mysterious became the sources of his nature and his being.

■ And what of Michael himself? I don't know what diverts him more: us or the animals.

During the first weeks here he could not stop looking at us and touching us. He kept stroking my hair and Lev's beard—both gray—as if they were of some rare substance. Obviously he had never seen gray hair before. With his long fingers he would trace the lines in our faces as if he were blind.

He became, in a way that touched and amazed us, a natural servant. The word has so long been in bad odor as the badge of inferiority and exploitation that perhaps I should say instead "one who serves." He became Barney's helper in the garden and the house, instinctively wise with tools as well as with growing things; and it was amazing to see how Barney's truculence evaporated in his presence.

He was fascinated by Annie's cooking, and he seemed to love preparing vegetables for her and even washing up. As for Annie, her long-suppressed maternal instincts rose to cherish him, all the more because Michael was afflicted. Barney kept telling her she was spoiling him, that he'd turn into a monster, but she would only smile and wave him away with her hand.

With Lev and Joey, it was much more complicated. He was a young man in full vigor and beauty, and for the first time they were made to feel old. Lev especially, with his vanity, grew depressed and irritable and the rest of us had to keep telling him how splendid he looked with his beard (which he did), how beautifully he played, to keep him from souring.

Stupid as it may sound, and pretentious for me, I think Joey was jealous. We had become very close in all ways and the fact that I could not hide the boy's fascination for me hurt Joey even though he was sensitive enough to know its origin.

Merely because Michael was a young man he reminded me of Ben and Sam, and like Annie I became his mother. More than that—and I was forced to admit it to myself—the thought of him as a lover was, however grotesque in the circumstances, never very far away. If you love men you can never remain oblivious of their bodies. Michael was hard of muscle and smooth of skin, his hair sprung from his head and circled his mouth with a baroque vigor, and it was impossible not to imagine, and desire. This maternal-erotic mixture—so old, so known—had always seemed obscene to me, and it still did. But there it was, unsettling and unresolved.

And then, always, there was the question of how much he knew, how much he heard, what he was thinking. We assumed that dumbness and deafness were interrelated: that you could speak (provided you had a tongue and palate) if you could hear. Michael very often smiled when we laughed and frowned when we were intense, but that proved nothing except an imitative sense which we found to be highly developed in

[149]

him. He would walk like Barney and gesture like Lev with uncanny—and convulsing—accuracy: a Marcel Marceau without the white mask.

Sometimes he would pick up books and even musical scores and seem to study them intently, and the fact that he chose to listen whenever Lev and Joey played convinced them that something must be getting through, must be affecting him.

But what? He would sit on the floor cross-legged, for music and much of talk, and at first this silent attention without response disturbed us, made us self-conscious, almost inhibited. We agreed that it was a little like being on television, speaking alone or on panel shows. You didn't know, you couldn't see, who you were talking to, you had no feedback. You talked into the blackness beyond the lights, and it always took a while before you could simply be yourself, speaking as you would in a room with others.

Michael was the eye of the camera, the ear of the darkness. We would just have to believe that he was hearing, and be as we were.

It wasn't easy, because we spent most of the time when he was with us speculating about him, and most of the time when he was out of earshot talking about him.

His room was a small one in the top of the round tower, with a cot, a chair, dresser, and a fine view of the fields and sea. But Michael slept on the ground on a blanket except in rain or heavy wind, and for the most part stayed outdoors rather than in. We worried constantly about him going too far afield and getting picked up by a patrol, and for the first weeks every time we saw one passing by we would hurry to find him, point at it, and shake our heads vehemently. He would shake his head too and frown like us.

Very often he would bring back from his roamings a live bird or a rabbit or a vole to show us, and how he managed to catch them we never knew. Nor did we know how he managed to train By and Phu not to harm them in his presence. He would keep the wild things only a short while and then release them, and we had the uncanny feeling that he could talk to the small ones as well as the bigger.

More and more we abandoned the theory of his having "escaped" from some institution.

"He is simply not of our time," said Lev one day. "He seems to have had nothing to do with this civilization."

I was sure that he had extrasensory perception. "His senses are certainly far more developed than ours, or he has more than five."

"No antennae!" said Joey. "Anyhow he's too big for a saucer."

"Not for a *big* saucer," said Annie, who believed in them implicitly.

"Look," said Barney, "he's a nice dumb kid who escaped from a love-in—"

"And walked into another," said Joey.

We laughed.

■ But we were serious when we got on the question of Michael's color. We were not at all sure that it was the result of long exposure to the sun. It had the uniform tone and texture of a basic pigmentation.

We agreed that his features were certainly not African, that he walked like a free man, and that he seemed singularly

[151]

without hate or rancor. He could not have come from any city of the United States as we knew them when the big troubles started. We had talked endlessly about what might have happened in the decade or more since we left, and could not understand why there were no Negroes in the Center.

Had the whole process of integration indeed been reversed, could they possibly in this short time have formed a black autonomous state, and if so where? Handing them Mississippi, Alabama, and Georgia would have seemed just retribution, but Joey felt that Texas would be even better.

They could at least have a sound economic base with the oil, and plenty of room.

We might joke now and then simply because the alternatives were so grim. The martial footing that served as the basis for our initial exile and seemed to have been steadily reinforced in the last year might be not only for external war but for civil war. With generation against generation and race against race, who could survive? Who would want to survive?

Ironically, our removal from the active world had spared us so far from violent confrontation. So far.

But if Michael were a Negro, why did he leave? Could he have fled from the militants because he couldn't be one of them?

"Forget it," said Joey. "For one thing this boy is no product of the ghettos or tenant farms. He's never been humiliated or kicked around. If he had, he'd hate our guts instead of working for us—voluntarily."

So we got back to where we started. Michael was the blessed idiot of Russian fable, of old folk legend.

Michael was not only dumb. He was insane.

[152]

■ "We were speaking," said Lev one evening devoted to an Article, "about those values which we still cling to and which had become dirty words to Them. We spoke of discipline and responsibility and dignity and grace. Well, it has occurred to me that they have become dirty words to the Negroes also."

"For different reasons," said Joey. "They are hardly the natural products of slavery."

"They are not natural products of anything," said Lev. "They must be taught."

"To free men," said Joey.

"Balls!" said Barney. "If we're talking about whites, what was freer than those rich colleges kids making like maniacs on Florida beaches with their goddamn beer cans? What about the Hippie parasites on dirty pads? Discipline? Dignity? Grace? You make me puke."

"Are we at least agreed," I said, "that they are desirable qualities?"

Joey muttered "in others" and I ignored him.

"Whether they are desirable to you or me," said Lev, "is not the point. They are essential to any civilized society—black or white."

"What about black *and* white?" said Barney.

"That," said Lev, "is what I was coming to."

LEV: You mix the affluence of the white and the poverty of the black and you do not get a civilized society. Integration on an equal level is one thing. Mixing on an unequal level is another. That is what was happening in the last years. The Negroes wanted all the privileges the rich whites had, without the capacity to achieve them. The whites wanted all the

[153]

privileges the Negroes had without the condition that be-stowed them.

JOEY: What the hell do you mean, "Negro privileges"? What "condition"?

LEV: It should be clear . . . the condition of the powerless victim. If you are that, you have no responsibility for what you are or do, you live only for the day, you have no future for which to build, no self-disciplines to apply, no inhibitions to say No! and you hate the society in which you live.

"These are precisely the luxuries many young whites bor-rowed from Negroes without the painful heritage that pro-duced them. And the Negroes, on the other hand, wanted all the money and status and luxuries the whites had without the years of effort and responsibility that brought them about."

We all jumped down Lev's throat on that and there was a loud overlapping wrangle, which can be contracted mainly to this: far too many whites got these luxuries not through effort and discipline but through chiseling, deals, and gambles, and it was to these models that the most deprived Negroes turned. "They got it quick, why shouldn't we?" was the fuse. Ironically, we argued, it was the "sharp" Negroes modeled on the chiseling whites who were applauded by the most militant blacks, while those who pulled themselves up with immense labor and pride to positions of trust and prominence drew contempt: they had joined Whitey.

LEV: You are only proving my point, which is that this process—this cross-pollination of the worst rather than the best—has been responsible for the over-all vulgarization and brutaliza-tion of our society, black and white. The loss of dignity, of discipline, and grace that were the mark of the slave are now the mark of the free.

We now share in common the most common of values.

JOEY: Lev, let's pull it out in the open once and for all. You are, you have been, and you always will be prejudiced.

LEV: Dear fellow, of *course* I am prejudiced! I am prejudiced against vulgar and violent people, I have never made a secret of that.

We told him he couldn't get away with that: he was prejudiced against Negroes as a race. "Not that you're alone," said Joey. "A hell of a lot of so-called enlightened whites kidded themselves that they weren't, and I knew plenty of these liberals who worked for civil rights and all that and then took their kids out of public school because they quote "weren't getting a good education in that neighborhood." And then he added, "I did it myself. The school my kids went to on the West Side was already over half Negro and Puerto Rican. The poor goddamn teachers did their best, which got them nowhere, and the kids didn't learn anything."

ANNIE: Lev is right. It is not the skin, it is the education people have.

BARNEY: It isn't the skin, it's the Afric features whites really hate, in their guts. What the hell can you expect when we've been brought up for centuries with a pale blond Christ and the Greek concept of beauty? Michael's dark enough to pass in Harlem, but he's got the features of a Masaccio duke! Jesus, I've painted pure African black women who were magnificent —could've been queens of Egypt, black goddesses. White men are plenty happy to screw them, but that's about it.

Joey started to pitch in, but Lev, inexorable, raised his voice and overrode him.

LEV: I feel no prejudice whatsoever against those who have managed to overcome—with enormous effort—what their past and white America has done to them. As you can imagine, I came into frequent contact with the finest Negro musicians, a few of whom are vastly superior to whites, especially the singers. There was no barrier at all between us, and I am sure the same feeling of total equality would exist with intelligent and cultivated Negroes of all professions . . . if we had ever had a chance to live beside them.

JOEY: If we'd started doing something two hundred years ago there'd be a hell of a lot more of them to feel equal with!

LEV: We! We! *I* did not import them as slaves, *you* did not import them as slaves and lynch them and oppress them, why should *we* be expected to bear the total responsibility for their condition?

K: Because any society bears a collective responsibility for any part of that society.

LEV: I said *total!* Of course we are responsible, let us say seventy, even eighty per cent responsible! But before and during the great violences the Negro flatly repudiated any part of the responsibility, however small! They had made a virtue of irresponsibility, and therefore they are no better than the fat white bullies of the South and the dreadful white women screamers of the North!

K: Look, we've been over all this again and again—

BARNEY: Why the hell not? We couldn't say any of this out loud before without being called a bigot by the blacks or a brother by the white bastard bigots. Talk about a free society! We were stuffed with fucking lies on both sides for centuries!

K: The "white bastard bigots" were brought up on lies. They're the product of a lousy education in humanity—or no education at all. If they were intelligent enough to know this, they could say they were not responsible for what they did either.

LEV: Thank God we are on the track again. My whole point in all this has been that the minute people justify their acts on the grounds that because of what was done to them—or *not* done *for* them—they are *not* responsible for their condition or their actions, you no longer have a civilized society. It is like saying that because you had a terrible mother who beat you, you are justified in beating women.

JOEY: Do unto others what they have done unto you.

LEV: The barbarian code. In black or white.

Michael came in at that point, smiled, and sat cross-legged on the floor. It was well-timed because the moment we got on race we went around and around in circles and proved nothing, except, perhaps that:

We were too far from events to know what was happening now.

We were the last of a society brought up on predominantly white, Christian, humanistic Western values, and therefore unequipped to cope with a multi-racial world that shared none of them.

We had a common revulsion against the violent primitivism of this new world, which an intellectual and moral understanding of it could not dispel.

We shared a deep underlay of guilt, not for what we had done but for what we might have failed to do; and, more than anything, for the shameful relief that we were now—by freak circumstance—spared from responsibility.

God knows what havoc They were still facing—black and white.

[157]

■ One night, a heavy rain drumming on the roof and eaves, we tried to pin down our Article on the blessed trinity, or what we felt were three of the pillars that propped up civilized life: Discipline, Grace, Responsibility.

It was the progressive disappearance of them—and in Them that had perhaps caused us the greatest pain and dislocation during the last years of our contact with normal living.

We decided to split Discipline into the two areas of manner and mind, and start with the first because it was easier.

LEV: Certainly not different. It all starts in the mind.

ANNIE: I don't agree. It is a habit to have manners, to behave in certain ways.

JOEY: Sure, but you have to be taught in the first place. Somebody tells you, "Do this, do that."

K: Certain things were drilled into us when we were children. Sometimes we rebelled against them, but after a while they became automatic, like saying "Please" and "Thank you" and "Excuse me."

BARNEY: Christ, whenever I heard anybody say that in New York, I broke down and cried.

JOEY: You mean like once a year.

K: The young think that's all part of the dishonesty, the lies we lived by. They said it didn't mean anything, it was a hollow form.

JOEY: I'd much rather have a hollow "Hello" than an honest "Fuck you!"

After similar diversions we finally got down to what kind of disciplines we would impose and who would impose them. And then, together, we decided to project a school that would redress

[158]

the enormous lacks in the system as we remembered it and somehow replace knowledge, which was crammed unremittingly into the heads of the young, with wisdom, which was quite another thing.

LEV: They should wear uniforms until college.

Shrieks of heresy! Reaction! Regimentation! Conformity! What about freedom? Individuality? Self-expression? The cornerstones of our democratic society!

Lev waved for quiet with his elegant hands.

LEV: Freedom is in here (tapping his head). Individuality you are born with. Have you ever seen the faces of nuns? They stand out more clearly simply because they *have* the same frame.

JOEY: What about soldiers?

LEV: Wouldn't you recognize your son in a line of them?

K: I agree with Lev about the girls. (They looked at me with astonishment). Yes, I mean it. I've thought for a long while that because of the fashion racket and the cosmetic racket girls thought much too much about how they looked instead of what they were. They started working for the sex and marriage market from the age of six on.

BARNEY: Why didn't you write that for your crappy magazine?

K: Ever heard of advertisers?

JOEY: But my God, Kate, you wouldn't want them to wear those atrocities that English girls used to wear when we were kids?

K: Of course not. I'm thinking of the kind of clothes Asian girls and women wear—at all ages. Those beautiful Vietnamese girls—remember?—with their long tunics and wrapped skirts or pants?

JOEY: Do I not! But that's the girl, not the clothes.

K: That's just what I'm getting at. The clothes—the same clothes, for all of them—brought out their difference. It didn't obscure them.

JOEY: Kate, our chicks would never buy that. What'd they do with their dough?

K: That's just what I'm getting at. The money would go to other things. We'd have a sort of Order of Poverty . . .

JOEY: Not chastity, I hope?

LEV: What is that?

K: I'm serious. Common poverty might be the only thing that would pull us together. All of us. I hate to say it but we need a catastrophe—a real one—to get back to basics.

JOEY: My God, she asks for a catastrophe! What do you think's going on now?

LEV: Just what *is* going on now?

JOEY: What's going on now is that *you* want to put the boys in uniform, for God's sake!

LEV: I do. It gives them a sense of importance, of dignity. They stand up straighter.

ANNIE: Like the Hitler youth?

JOEY: Lev, she's right. I don't know about the girls, ha ha, but with males doesn't that kind of regimentation always make for brainwashing?

BARNEY: No more than the business suit, for Christ's sake. What makes you think Americans aren't brainwashed, Joey? "God bless free enterprise and if you're against it you're a fucking Communist!"

K: Look, none of us are thinking of stiff collars and brass buttons. I'm thinking more of the kind of clothes workmen wore to work, depending on what they did. Telephone linesmen, construction workers, doctors, astronauts. Clothes right for the job.

JOEY: In this case the job of learning?

LEV: The job of concentrating on larger issues than money —hence status, hence clothes, hence the idiocy of an unlimited consumer economy in a starving world.

JOEY: Let us pray.

LEV: You can laugh, but why do you suppose we have managed to survive as well as we have here? Because by an accident of fate we have been deprived of all those superfluities that we were told were essential! Because we have learned to live without *things!*

JOEY: Lev, I never thought I'd hear you spout the Hippie line!

ANNIE: But we have luxuries.

K: We have what They haven't got, Lev. Privacy . . . space . . .

BARNEY: And talent, goddamnit. Even Annie here . . .

ANNIE: Thank you.

JOEY: Hippies had no talent. They just lay around with flowers in their ears.

K: Look, we were starting a school, see? We were putting the kids in uniform . . .

BARNEY: We were caning the little bastards . . .

LEV: Ah yes, discipline . . . discipline, above all!

■ The talk of "uniforms" has reminded me that I've hardly mentioned clothes during all this time simply because they had become so unimportant.

Not that we ceased to care how we looked: we were all

[161]

acutely aware of the danger of not caring; of an external slovenliness that inevitably reflected internal sickness. But as the clothes we came with wore out and the ones available at the Center were sleazy and shapeless (since when had They ever designed for the old?), we made our own.

This is not quite accurate. Annie, as talented in sewing as she was in cooking, made them for us with the allotments of mill-end yardage that we were permitted to buy during the first years for curtains, covers, and whatever concessions to normal living They made for us.

We found after trial and error that one kind of "uniform" succeeded best for the life we led and the people we had become. Except for Annie, who was happiest in loose shifts, the rest of us wore slacks and tunics, which were really not very different from the Chinese Communist costume or the Russian high-collared shirt of czarist days. They escaped drabness by different colors and different closings (front or side for the tunics) and different heights of collars. They covered our aging skin, they left us free in movement, and they were nearly indestructible.

Even before we were put away, I had always felt that there was something both trivial and obscene in the preoccupation among older women about clothes. It was, of course, part of the insanity of "youth" that affected us all, that left us no choice but to look as They looked by wearing what They wore: a fallacy that made fools of most women over forty for quite a while.

Equally obscene was the preoccupation with fashion for the female child. Surely, I thought, there must be two stages of life free from this tyranny of externals: youth and age. The bodies of boys and girls spoke for themselves: they brought beauty to anything. As for men and women in their final span, however vigorous, their minds and hearts were their adornments.

In between, in the contest of identities, let them wear their war paint if they must and assert their colors.

If this hint of uniformity—or uniform—creeps into this account from time to time and suggests the kind of thinking common to regulated, collective societies, so be it. To us who had seen the progressive breakdown of the totally "free" society, of the individual pursuit of pleasure and profit, socialism was not a fearsome word, nor were certain aspects of the Communist states without worth.

One of these—and we had talked of it often—was the sense of common purpose, of common pride, that the competitive life seldom managed to produce. If this sense of spiritual community could be advanced by obliterating the standard insignia of rank or condition—if these disciplines (the habits and orders of a religious body) could be maintained without a shackling uniformity of mind—did they not have value?

Wasn't it about time that we addressed ourselves more to inner rather than outer space?

■ Having just looked at the last sentence, I am compelled to confess that I still address myself to the outer space that is my skin and body. Having once been beautiful I cannot bear to be ugly.

So although a change in A.A. policy for the last years made the cosmetics and hormones we used to buy unavailable (as life-prolonging), Annie and I concocted all sorts of things, from fats to keep our skin from drying to lemons and egg white to keep it taut. They were not appetizing, but they helped.

If swimming was impossible because of cold or roughness, I did daily exercises—very brief but comprehensive. We had long suspected that rigidity of mind or body was the real enemy of life, and that one state nearly always invited the other. There seemed no question that both had been slowly killing Barney. Or, conversely, that our exercises of thought and tissue had been largely responsible for keeping the rest of us going.

So too—and this was important—was the freedom from the relentless impingements and pressures suffered by those in the world: from crowds and pollution and buying and selling and competing, from the continuous stream of messages, heard and seen; from Total Information. I suppose no prisoners were ever more liberated, from what had in effect become a massive psychic as well as physical pollution.

Barney and I continue to be fascinated by the calligraphy of birds on the sand. He spells it "gra-feetie"; (he is childishly proud of his puns).

Anyway, the patterns of their claws on the beach are beautiful, humorous, and mysterious. The forked prints, so tiny of terns and sandpipers, so forthright and stolid of gulls, weave in and out, march straight, overlap, form circles, trample thickly around a dead fish or a piece of seaweed, trail off, vanish on the edges of wetness.

Sometimes the tracks approach in single file, meet, tramp, scrabble; to what? A confrontation? Love? An argument?

Sometimes you see the pheasant signature: two claws and

the faint dragging line of spur. What is he doing on the beach? What, no cover?

They have their life. Simpler than ours, but not so simple as all that.

Except, perhaps, to Michael, who has covered pages and pages with their prints as if they were a language, to be read. Which of course, it is—to those who can read it.

I forgot another calligraphy. One blade of shore grass, spear-tip bent and blown by the wind, traces a perfect circle in the sand. No compass could do better.

Design—pattern—order. Who needs more evidence?

■ We talk a lot about discipline but we are practicing it less and less.

One by one we have dropped out of our games-for-the-preservation-of-self—the Blind Days and Deaf Days and so forth—for one reason or another.

Lev complains of bursitis in one shoulder, Joey claims he hears perfectly with his eyes open, and Barney worries us all deeply with his growing disabilities.

His arthritis seems worse, his voice certainly is, and Annie, though calm and tender with him, is frantic with us.

"We must *do* something," she keeps saying, "we must *do* something before They come." We are sure that the results of his last computer test will indicate terminal illness, and we spend much of our time scanning the roads beyond the fields for the dreaded white panel truck with the A.A. on it.

Joey and I still feel well physically, but we confess to ourselves that the elation of fighting this rear-guard battle, of being the last survivors of our time and defying *this* time, has begun to wear off.

We are still determined to leave some record of this battle behind us, though a sense of futility and waste dogs my fingers on this erratic typewriter, vintage and obsolete as we are.

■   I am the only one left who still swims in the sea.

Joey, city boy that he was, was never comfortable in it even on calm days when the water was temperate.

Until his lameness, Barney would walk the beach nearly every day but never get wet.

Annie loved the water, but only when her feet were on the sand. On days of foaming surf she would bob up and down on the edges of it like a child.

Only Lev was an ardent swimmer, not so much for love of sea as for love of his body. He knew what swimming did to muscle and tissue, and, unless it was extremely rough, he would count his hundred strokes a day as one more ritual of vanity. Only these last two months has be begun to skip them, and this week he did not go to the beach at all.

So I have been going alone, although Michael sometimes comes to look, to play with By. His long immersion seems to have frightened him: another mystery as he seems in such total harmony with his physical environment and such a master of it.

And now I too am a little afraid. Afraid of waves that used to be dares and challenges, afraid of being caught in currents or vortices, pulled down or carried out, rolled or bereft of breath. Afraid of what happens when the water is very cold and I watch my fingers turn white, a corpse's hand, without feeling until the blood runs back.

But it is still the postnatal fluid of my being, the life, the joy, the resurrection. Before I forget my physical affinity for open sea, I must try to recapture the feelings of our long union. It has to do with this narrative because it has to do with survival. It gives life to those who give themselves to it. (The cardinal principle, and Christ said it better.)

How do I love it? Playful, sage-green, with small peaked waves and ruffles, translucent and bouncing, full of interior light. The water hardly cooler than the blood, but enough to excite, refresh.

Sullen and towering, with massed battalions of breakers rolling in snarling with foam. Dive as the crest begins to curl on the concave wall, pull out as it pounds full force behind your feet. Bob there and swim in the safety zone, lifted high by each swell in a leap like a ballerina, weightless and free. This is a pas de deux, the sea and you, in rapturous fusion.

Prussian blue, hard-edged, flat as a lake in the offshore wind from the north. The water too cold, too shocking to the body; an exultant test.

So many tests, so many moods. So much power and so much gentleness.

It is the healer and the reviver, it cleanses the cavities of self-disgust and melancholy, of sloth and negation with the salt solution of life. It cures the lethargies of flesh and spirit with the slap and shake of elemental force. It cradles and comforts. Give it trust and it holds you secure; fight it and it kills.

There is no age in water, no weight. Embraced in fluid that has known extreme dark and extreme light, harbored innumerable beings in a realm without definition, favored innumerable shores, man himself is not measured by time or space, he is merely the sum of his will and force, of his own fluidity.

How often have I said to myself: so long as I can swim in the sea I am young; I am whole.

■ Two days after writing this I was badly rolled. Instead of looking seaward as I always did when I came in from the breakers, diving through them until my feet touched bottom and I could race the oncoming one to shore, I stopped to look at Michael making enormous leaps along the beach—so long, so high, I could only think of Nijinsky, who I once saw in Paris when I was a very small child.

And then the roaring water fell on me and ground me into the sand and flung me around and around like a sack. I couldn't get my head out of water to breathe, I was dragged and sucked backward and then thrown forward again, until Michael saw me and with By barking wildly at his side pulled me up to dry sand and watched me, dark with fear, until I caught my gasping, humiliated, frightened breath.

No age, I repeated to myself, no age. But I knew I was measured at last.

■ After Joey had scanned this passage he said, "Very fancy. Very sexy. Why don't you ever talk about *me* like that?"

"Like what? You're not an element."

"The hell I'm not. Don't I fall on you and fling you around like a sack?"

"A bag," I said. (Joey once countered my apologies for not

being young by saying "But I *like* fading bags! They're more comfortable, you can get a *grip* on them!")

"Okay, I fling you around like a fading bag!"

I had to laugh, but then Joey said in an uncharacteristically gentle voice, "Kate—don't ever go in a sea like that again. Ever. It had nothing to do with age, nothing at all."

I let him comfort me, but of course I knew better.

■ Only one thing has happened lately to restore our will and excitement.

As I write, Michael spends most of his nights outdoors, on a blanket on the rough grass.

This afternoon he brought a piece of paper—the kind Barney uses to draw on—to Barney, who looked at it closely for a while and then came hobbling in to show it to me, the boy following.

It seemed at first like a lot of dots. But these dots—and clusters of dots—were in several places connected by faint lines, which formed—clearly and discernibly—the shapes of animals and, in one instance, a man.

There was a bear, there was a swan—"My God," I said, "constellations!"

Seeing our rapt faces turn to him, Michael smiled, pointed upward, and then began to imitate a bear and a swan.

Barney was excited chiefly by the quality of his observation and line, the rest of us—I interrupted Joey and Lev (still playing, thank God)—to show it to them, fascinated by his archaic interpretation of the stars.

Where did he learn it? When?

We had no answers, but Barney at last had a pupil. If only it had happened earlier I think it might have added years to his life, for I was sure that much of Barney's rage at being no longer needed or wanted as an artist had turned inward on his cells and tissues: the wild inverted growth that is the opposite of birth.

Already because of his aching legs and back, Barney had turned most of his gardening chores over to the youth, but that tutelage was an abdication. This new one was not. It was a resumption of the authority he had long since lost except in the drawings he still made of the natural world for his own pleasure.

These he showed to Michael, to whom he then brought a series of objects—fruits, stones, mushrooms, weeds—telling him to draw them.

Michael did, but with a fussiness of line unlike his constellation drawings. Discussing them one night in his absence, we could only assume that he had seen ancient astronomical charts in some book and been made to copy them accurately. We could not, however, imagine any existent school that would require him to.

In any case, Barney managed to impart in him an accuracy of vision and an economy of line that was startlingly effective. The boy's coordination was clearly fantastic; there were none of the interior barriers or obstructions caused by previous conditioning to come between eye and hand.

But these were mere exercises. Michael's sights were turned on something far higher.

We knew that he had a passion for the electric car that bordered on veneration. He could not stop examining it, feeling it, patting it, and cleaning it. It had never gleamed so before, and his tender zeal amused us, although even in a young man of this technological age it seemed excessive.

Doubly so when we saw a large wreath of wild flowers and leaves encircling its radiator one morning, and Michael sitting on the ground drawing it.

"Sacred cow," said Joey. "Whaddaya know!"

■ Michael had given the sacred cow a face, comic and sinister. Not a real face, but an arrangement of parts that suggested one.

In this he and I were alike. I was always seeing faces in everything: human or animal faces in stones, pieces of wood, tree trunks, clouds. It is not anthropomorphic, for it is not God I see in everything but a common humanity, which some, for that matter, might call God.

Whatever it is, it invests the inanimate, or presumed inanimate, with feeling: a stricken tree, a torn branch, a broken flower; there is pain in their fracture. I am sure this is so with Michael, in the way he handles living things, in the way he handles a bird with a broken wing.

He even feels for those armored tanks of the sea, the horseshoe crabs. If he sees one turned impotent on its back, its ugly legs still scrabbling upward, he picks it up by its spiny tail and turns it over and tosses it into the water, waiting until it has purchase on the sand below and then moved outward under the froth.

But I see something else that I'm sure Michael doesn't see. I see death in objects that never had life. Far off I see a dead bird and it is only a piece of crumpled tin. On the road I see a small dead animal—a cat? a dog? a muskrat?—and it is only a piece of wrapping paper or an old burlap bag.

Is it eyes? Is it age? Is it the slow conditioning for death?

Or is it the pervasive sense of pain and compassion that all life stirs in me even when I celebrate beauty?

Sometimes I think it is a kind of insanity to feel for everything, with everything, to this degree. If it is, it does less harm than the sanity that sanctions killing, for whatever presumed ends.

■ I have finally tried to come to grips with the next to last Article, although we haven't been able to agree on a name for it. It has to do with Discipline and Grace and Responsibility, it has to do with Sensibility and Ethics, with the training in these qualities, with the early conditioning of the young. I suppose Education is the word for it. None of us, though, except Lev, like the word, which is a commentary on what has been done in its name.

There was plenty of disagreement along the line, Lev holding more to a rigid classical curriculum at an earlier age, the rest of us more flexible in our priorities.

Number one of these was that children from about the ages of four to ten should be educated exclusively in the use of their senses, and in a sense of humanity. The cultivation of the human organism and the cultivation of the human conscience should come before the training of the intellect. Without an understanding of the world inside them they could not truly perceive the world outside them. And vice-versa.

We were all sitting or sprawling in this world outside that particular day: again, one of the rare ones without wind. A flotilla of fluffy white clouds barely moved in the candid sky and the birds were particularly loud in the depths of the bushes. A purple finch was at the feeder, two female cardinals were beneath it pecking at seeds. In the far corner of this grassy space a very small rabbit cropped grass, his nose trembling, his head lifted every half second for possible threat. Michael was stretched on his stomach on the ground sketching him.

We were all, for once, reduced to silence by the exquisite texture of this day, this hour; more than ever aware, I was sure, that it was one of our last and that its benediction must be wholly savored. Oh love, oh joy, oh peace, I wanted to cry; what have we done to it on this planet? What have we done?

Finally Annie broke the silence. "They should have respect for all living things—like Michael."

"*They* don't," growled Barney, pointing a gnarled finger at the rabbit. "Eat the bloody tops off my flowers!"

"Oh, Barney, we're not talking about your flowers, we're talking about children!"

Lev said, "Come now, Annie, you don't want the children to have respect for *all* living things. They should detest the barbarians."

"Our definition of barbarians, of course," I said.

L E V : Of course! There are absolute values of good and evil, and the sooner They learn this the more hope there is for the race, if there is any left. You will remember, I trust, that before we left, the most popular intellectuals gave the mob the perfect excuse for license. They said there *were* no absolute values. Good and evil, right and wrong were subjective judgments, and people who performed antisocial acts were sick.

B A R N E Y : Or revolutionaries.

J O E Y : Or underprivileged.

K : We've gone into that before.

L E V : We must go into it *again*. If a man loots, he is a thief, if a man burns a house, he is an arsonist. If a man rapes, he is a rapist. I don't care where he comes from, what color he is, or what background he had. He has performed crimes for which *he alone*—nobody else, no group, no history—is responsible.

K: You don't believe in collective guilt?

LEV: Of course I do. What I do not believe in is collective excuse, as I said before.

JOEY: Okay, so how you going to knock that into the young without religion? When I last looked, God was dead.

K: You can teach ethics without religion. My parents did.

BARNEY: Remember all that fuss about those goddamn school prayers? All the little bastards mumbling My Father Who Art every day and then playing dirty in the school yard? Some people even thought that saying "I pledge allegiance to my flag and blah blah" made you a patriot.

JOEY: It seems to me that the only way you're going to knock ethics into people is to show 'em that whatever anybody does affects everybody.

K: Apparently the Soviets do that in their kindergartens. Or did. The children were in various groups. When one of their group did something wrong, all the rest shared his guilt and had their privileges withheld. And when one of them did something very good, they all were given a special treat.

JOEY: Pure adulterated socialism!

BARNEY: What the hell do you think we're living in now?

JOEY: Here or outside?

BARNEY: Both, natch. Only good thing They ever did: change the bloody systems we had.

LEV: Do you mean by kicking us out of it?

K: Look, we're talking about the kids—not about us.

ANNIE: Sometimes it is the same.

LEV: We were talking, I believe, about the training of

conscience, the fact that you cannot build this into children without a strict code of ethics, or the principles of human duty.

K : These principles being absolute.

JOEY : What happened to that fellow who said "Thou shalt not kill, thou shalt honor thy father and thy mother, thou . . ."

LEV : Shalt not commit adultery.

JOEY : I guess it isn't what you would call a "fun philosophy." Can you imagine making a movie out of it?

BARNEY : They did. Awful Bible crap. All those people in white gowns and beards.

JOEY : Funny. When we were around, a whole generation of kids was brought up on murder, adultery, crime—Everything Goes . . . or went. But They weren't the ones who bombed hell out of little countries to bring them democracy.

LEV : Maybe They are now. They are old enough to think like their fathers.

ANNIE : Their fathers were not taught to feel the bombs on themselves. You cannot know what you do not feel.

■ This remark of Annie's set us back on the track again, because it tied up the senses and the conscience, where we had started. So we laid down a sort of curriculum for the young that went this way:

They should have, as we did, their Blind Days, their Deaf Days, their Dumb Days, their Crippled Days, so that they would not only understand affliction in others but learn the primacy of their own five senses.

Assuming that there was any wilderness left, those over eight should spend at least two weeks a year, in groups of not more than twenty, in direct confrontation with nature and with only minimal equipment for survival. There were, we remembered, such "survival" courses here and there in which older youths were put through rigorous paces and tests of endurance in remote places, and we felt these should be compulsory experiences for the majority.

Even more, they must go without food or shelter for a three-day period to gain some understanding of what half of the world endured most of the time.

For much the same reason—to diminish at least somewhat the great and demonstrably dangerous gap between rich and poor—there should be instituted a Minimum Basic Allowance for all children, regardless of the economic status of their parents. They could then not confuse the establishment of identity with the consumption of goods. What you were, in short, in no way depended on what you had.

"Who's gonna compulse?" said Joey at this point. "Who's gonna make kids do these things? They won't buy it. I wouldn't, God knows. Christ—no money, no comfort, no *food?*"

"Joey," said Lev patiently, "we are speaking of an ideal education of children of a spoiled and formless society that cannot survive without drastic change."

I said it was just possible that the compulsion would come from actual privation—from catastrophe—if it were not state-induced.

"A little tyranny," said Lev, "would be very salutary at this point . . . at least for the young. The results of total freedom have not been very edifying."

"The results of dictatorship," said Joey to Lev, "are considerably less edifying. Hell, you can't decree ethics . . . or conscience. That's bullshit."

We finally decided that it was a question of imagination.

If you could imagine the result of certain acts—of violence, of cruelty, of indifference—if you could be made to follow them through to their ultimate conclusions—you would not perform them; or stand by while they were performed.

In our "school," children would be shown what a bullet actually does to the body, what a heavy blow does to the brain, what a fire bomb does to the flesh, what starvation does to a child's belly, how dogma can lead to death. At regular intervals from the age of ten onward, the young would be made to see what wars have done—and undone.

"They must be taught to be gentle," said Annie. This led us to the lost word "gentleman." Were we in fact all in our own ways proposing the preposterous: the education of gentle people? (Flower-people, if you will, but with direction and control?)

At this point Barney limped out muttering profanely something about the worst bitches he'd ever known were ladies; Joey said gentlemen were the products of privilege and now everybody was equal, but Lev and I insisted that gentle people were not the products of class but of training and that all the things we were talking about—Discipline, Grace, Responsibility, and so forth—could be learned.

"But for what purpose? What carrot do you hold out to kids to make 'em learn? Gentlemen don't make money, they don't make the big time—they don't make revolution—what the hell's *in* it for them?"

"Pleasure in living," said Lev. "The reduction of friction. A sense of order . . ."

Again and again we came back to that word; to order, pattern, frame, form. Without it life was not worth living. But what frame, what order?

The nine-to-five frame of man-at-office, woman-at-home, separated for ten hours a day? The order of houses on a sterile suburban street, with two nestling bushes and unused, useless lawn? The pattern of money and things and more things? The order of battle lines and lying words? The form of fission? Wasn't all this, we came to conclude, precisely what drove Them from us? And weren't They justified?

I said we were talking about education in gentleness: of social forms that didn't necessarily make better people but certainly made for a better life.

"There was," said Lev, "in my youth something they called deportment. My sister had lessons in it at school, where she was taught how to sit, how to walk, how to stand erect, how to greet people, even how to entertain."

I said that was done in the so-called finishing schools of my youth, which I had derided. But my own mother taught me to stand straight and sit tranquilly, to rise for elders, and to sing for my supper.

"Meaning exactly what?" asked Joey.

Meaning that if I were asked to a social gathering I had an obligation to contribute to it. Meaning that if I gave one I had an obligation to see that no one was bored or ignored.

"Meaning," said Lev, "that it was considered a human obligation to give pleasure to others."

"Man," said Joey, "that's a revolutionary theory! Don't you know that's considered just about the worst crime on Their list? Give *pleasure*? To *please*? Christ, that was the dirtiest thing you could say about anything from a play to a picture. Please yourself, okay, but fuck everybody else!"

I asked him whether he was standing in for Barney, but we agreed that the pleasure principle—as the new breed would have it—was confined exclusively to self, and not available for export. That two generations, whether they were prominent intellectuals or checkout boys in supermarkets, had grown up contemptuous of amenities.

JOEY: Somebody took me to a writers' party on Riverside Drive, I'll never forget it. There were all these big names sitting around drinking, I didn't know which dame was the hostess, some creep pointed out the bar, and that was about it. Nobody gave a damn about me—too "popular," I guess, to be important, they all talked book-talk to each other while the dames stroked their curly heads and got fried. I finally found some half-naked doll who looked promising, but turned out she was a dyke who wrote criticism about criticism, so I got stoned and left. Never saw such a bunch of boors in my life.

K: Worse than musicans?

JOEY: Look, musicians may stink, but at least they can play.

ANNIE: Where we lived there was a stationer, he never took his cigar out of his mouth while he got you something.

LEV: Disgusting habit!

JOEY: Anal-erotic.

I suggested that, quite apart from social form, there was nothing left of the aesthetics of behavior. The cigar-mouthers and gum-chewers had no sense of their ugliness, they never really *saw* themselves—or, for that matter, others.

Barney had lumbered back. "Aesthetics! God almighty, Kate, how do you expect people to see anything in a country where kids have never been taught to look! Why do you think we've made the ugliest towns in the world, why do you think our public buildings have been disasters and our private ones mostly frauds? Why do you think we've fucked up our whole country-

side with signs and wires and dump heaps and lousy develop-
ments? The *kids were never taught to see!"*

His vehemence made him cough again and Annie said,
"Please—don't try . . . please." It hurts us too to hear him now,
as it did to see him walk. But his rage—and strangely enough,
his rage to live—forced him on, and what use was there to make
him save himself now?

BARNEY : When they're kids, forget about the great masters
and show 'em the great mess! Make 'em look at what's around
them now in their cities and in their houses, make 'em touch
and draw and describe 'em, and if they like what they see or
don't like what they see, make 'em tell you why!

"Peel the film off their eyes and teach 'em to face the fact,
ugly or great! Then make 'em look through microscopes and
telescopes to see that the infinitesimal is just as goddamn
beautiful as the infinite, something the bloated painters of
square yards never knew.

"Make 'em look at the faces and bodies of their families and
their friends and learn what happens to a body, and be disgusted by Dad's belly lapping over his belt and Mom's flesh
shaking like Jello! Just so long as they *see* and know what
they're seeing, whether it's on a wall or a street or a page—on
television or whatever They've invented now to screw the eye!"

We waited for him while he coughed and took rough deep
breaths. We could barely hear him when he spoke again:

"When they're fifteen or so—then show 'em—show 'em
Leonardo's notebook . . . and take it from there. . . . Teach
'em never to believe the double-talkers . . . believe themselves.
Tell 'em art isn't for kicks, it's a matter of life and death . . .
gotta move your guts as well as your mind . . . gotta be in the
great line! Know what I mean? *Great line!"*

He tried to get up but fell back. Annie went to him and helped him and took him upstairs, very slowly, to his room. On the stairs she looked back briefly in a way that tore the heart.

On the floor by my feet By gave a shuddering sigh, raised his head, sat up, and rested his chin on my knee. Phu, on Lev's lap, began to speak his strange language but Lev put his hand over his muzzle and said, "Hush! Hush!" and the cat subsided.

■ If you who read this think we hated you—Them—you are wrong. We did at first, for how long I cannot say, for you hurt us greatly (we thought!), and our alienation was greater than any you had ever known or felt.

What did you expect, in any case? Your resentment of us could only have produced our equal resentment of you. You were the conquering enemy hordes from which we exempted only our own flesh and blood who—we rationalized—had been helplessly seduced or betrayed.

But this was at first. Later, removed so long from your presence, our longing for the sight of you matched our silence in confessing it to each other. It was, I suppose, a matter of pride. By God, if you didn't want us, we didn't want you. We would show Them how we could live without Them—without you.

Well, we did. And the more we managed not only to defy our fate but to alter it in our own image, the more we discovered two things.

One was the deprivation of your physical presence. On our walks on a summer beach in simmering heat Annie and I (we admitted later) peopled it with the bodies of children: the little boys with their splayed fingers and thrust bellies, the little girls with their downy hair and thrusting rears.

We saw the older ones (how we hated the word "teen-agers"!) with their long beautiful legs and shining skin, diving into the waves and out again, with streaming hair on wet and laughing faces. (The commercials for soaps, I thought with a twist of contempt; or selling nothing? What did it matter?)

And Joey sometimes would talk of Them, of you, saying God, they were beautiful, those girls, with their faces like Madonnas and their skirts up to their crotches! And I thought, but never said: God, they are beautiful, young men with their sullen mouths and their waving hair: Gawain or Lancelot!

But along with this physical deprivation—of vital flesh and flashing motion, of the young animal—there was something else, something profoundly ironic that emerged one night—in what context I can't remember. I don't even remember who said—out of the blue—"You know, we're living like Them!"

And the more we thought about it, the truer it seemed. At least, we bore a strong resemblance to those of you (then often reviled) who had found a way of life in sharp variance from the so-called norm of society or what were then known as "middle-class values." We were, Joey said, "Clean Hippies."

For one thing, we were bound together not by blood but by mutuality of circumstance and feeling. We were a community, not a family. We admitted that as a family—in tension or monotony—we could never have survived this exile and isolation.

Money, clothes, possessions had ceased to matter. The fact that They voluntarily renounced them, while we were compelled to, made little difference. We had shelter, a piano (substitute guitar), and each other.

We were not beggars, but we lived on others: on state money, on welfare. We did not work for others.

Though we existed in an artificial system we lived in a natural world. We had freed our senses to become part of it. We had left ourselves open to feeling and to revelation.

We hated war and violence and in particular the kind of wars our leaders were waging and the kind of violence our people had rationalized. We had withdrawn (been forced to withdraw) from what had become a brutal and dishonest society.

We loved each other not because marriage or parenthood or legal ties expected it of us but out of mutual respect, common beliefs, and compassion. We shared profound doubts about the institution of marriage as it had been, and the perpetuation of the small family unit.

The family, the tribe, the nation were to us archaic terms. Only the family of man was now a valid concept.

We did not believe in the religion of science, the dogma of private enterprise, or the cult of technological progress. Competition as a spur and a system was anathema to us.

We were unrealistic in terms of present realities, but realistic in terms of future change.

We were denied responsibility (while the passive young abdicated from it) and were therefore powerless, politically and socially.

We retained power only over our own conscience.

We were radical.

We were an outcast minority.

We were nuts!

(*scrawled by Joey, who has just read all this.*)

The others reacted characteristically.

LEV: Very neat, very neat, Kate. But those you say we are like did not believe in the work or the virtue of work. We do, we always have. They do not live by codes or disciplines, they swim in a formless sea. We insist upon pattern or ritual, they exist through sensation alone.

JOEY: You keep forgetting one little thing: these kids we're talking about aren't the ones who took over. They're the ones who lost.

K: I said that. I said they were an outcast minority. So are we.

JOEY: Okay, but maybe those bells-and-beads kids turned into the cool computer cats that *did* take over!

BARNEY: Balls. The centurions took over. What the hell is this country now but an armed camp? The generals won.

But none of us really believed this. These were the last barks of old dogs defying ghosts they know are not there, or friends that they pretend are strangers. It was a matter of honor to keep on barking, as By does whenever Michael approaches.

■ As a respite from the Articles, which exhausted us, we played Speculation. What were They doing now, what was happening to our country.

These are some of the combined fancies that flowered from ignorance and irreverence:

The country was not just under temporary martial law, it had become a dictatorship. The dictator was:

The president of the National Rifle Association.

The national student-leader of the Radical Left.

A gangster in control of the entire drug market.

The inventor of the final weapon.

A black Maoist.

Negroes were now in control of all the major cities, although whites still ran what was left of the countryside.

The poor Negroes lived in the decayed central core of their cities, had poor schooling, and were badly treated by the Negro police force and discriminated against by the wealthy Negroes, who now occupied the best neighborhoods.

Alternately, the Negroes had formed a nation composed of those states where slavery had originated. The territory therefore included Louisiana, Alabama, Mississippi, Georgia, and South Carolina. This was called Blackland, and was a member of the United Nations.

Blackland was ruled by the extreme militants who had risen from the ranks of the rioters two decades or more ago. Many skilled and educated Negroes had defected from Blackland and sought asylum with the whites, who welcomed them. The defectors said there was torture, repression, and terrorism in Blackland and that they wanted to live in a free society where everyone was equal.

Many of these refugees, like those in the thirties from Germany and Austria, assumed positions of prominence in the intellectual, artistic, and economic life of the white society, of which they were part of the mainstream.

■ We were not always so frivolous. Most of us were in fact convinced that soon after we had been exiled there had been a year of racial guerrilla war and carnage in which many whites and Negroes had been killed and many parts of our cities laid waste. We assumed the final result to be a police state, a total freezing of attitudes on both sides, the death of humanism, and the final rout of liberals.

Our removal had spared us this, had probably even spared us what was left of our life. But even more, it had spared us the dreadful choice of taking sides. Faced with violent division we would have had to be not for humanity but for our race. And this was precisely the barbarism we despised.

What else but these divisions had ruined our world? Black/White, Right-Left, Reds/Us, Rich/Poor, Old/Young, Man/Woman—these were the fatal wars of stupidity. They had not only killed reason, but—by now—very possibly our own flesh and blood.

■ During this summer, now nearing autumn, Michael had been joining our discussions more and more. Again, we have no idea how much he understands, but there seems to be no question that he is comforted—as By and Phu are—by our physical presence and the sound of our voices.

Yet as Barney has been absenting himself often this month because of pain and the difficulty of speech, Michael has chosen to lie in the corridor upstairs outside his room and keep vigil at night. Annie has told him that he does not need to, that she is right opposite in case of need, but Michael merely smiles and shakes his head, and Annie is so touched that she doesn't press the point.

He continues to mystify us completely. Once (out of his hearing, of course) we even entertained the thought that he *might* have dropped out of a flying saucer into the sea.

Annie is convinced of this, she had always wanted to believe in saucers, and so—for that matter—had I. I maintained that he came from a star, or planet, where the state of civilization was Greco-Roman, certainly pre-Christian. I suggested he might be a slave, a thought that delighted Lev, the congenital master.

The men were quick to point out that a star as backward

as that of Michael's origin could hardly have reached the state of technology needed to transport him here.

The logic of this was difficult to refute, but not to dismiss.

Wherever Michael had come from, Annie and I stoutly maintained, it was not this world. And if he were a slave, he was freer than anyone we had ever known.

■ I am writing this because Kate hasn't been able to write since she killed By.

She's never said anything in this about how blind he was getting, and then something went wrong with his back legs, he sort of dragged himself along. None of us could say anything about it, and she wouldn't either. Everybody knew he was a very old dog, but now. . . .

Anyway, it's been a lousy week, fog every day. In the middle of it she went out with By toward the beach. I didn't see her go, thank God, because he could hardly walk now and wherever they went it must have taken a long time.

Anyway, she came back—I don't know how much later—and went to her room and locked herself in for the rest of the day. She must have been crying all that time, although you couldn't hear anything and she never does, usually. I went to the door and tried to get her to open up because I got scared she might do something to herself. But all she would say was "I'll be all right, don't worry."

But finally, around midnight, I tried again and then she opened, and of course she didn't say anything and neither did I. What can you say?

Poor goddamn dog.

J.

■ I'm grateful to Joey for writing that, but he got one thing wrong. I didn't go out with By. He went alone.

I spent the rest of the day looking for him, because I didn't see how he could go far in his condition and I was sure he'd hurt himself or was lying exhausted somewhere near the house or the beach.

I had thought of giving him a pill but couldn't bring myself to it.

Of course I asked everybody else if they'd seen him, but nobody had.

When I asked Michael he shook his head, and then put his hands to the side of his face and made the sleep gesture, his head to one side and his eyes closed.

Obviously he meant sleep, or death. But why was there no body?

In a way it's better. It's bad enough as it is.

■ Last night during dinner Joey said, "I wonder who has done more harm to the world—the people with tight minds or the people with loose minds?"

"Loose as in bowels—or marbles?" asked Barney.

"Well, the tight people think so. I meant sort of flexible—open—room at the top . . ."

"You are, perhaps," said Lev, "referring to liberals?"

So then we were off.

JOEY: I'm talking about the people who have room in their heads for new ideas. The tight ones—sure, call 'em constipated

—are all filled up. They want to hold onto everything they've got.

BARNEY: Back to bowels. Why the hell don't you spell it out? *They're* the bastards of the world—the reactionaries—the goddamn golfers with their fucking clubs!

(*Lev began to conduct and sing the "Internationale."*)

JOEY: You know he *has* something—the business of getting a little ball into a little hole—very tight. Very neat. And all that manicured grass. And the dear old poops riding around in their carts with little hats.

K: Liberals are more tennis types, maybe. Running all over the place—reaching high—slamming into the net.

LEV: So which type ruins the world?

ANNIE: It is childish.

JOEY: Maybe so, Annie. But out of the mouths of ba—

LEV: Liberal leads to radical leads to revolution leads to what?

BARNEY: The freedom of the masses! (He raised a clenched fist.)

LEV: And the asses?

JOEY: Sure, so what? So where do the tight brains lead?

K: Same thing. If there were no tight brains, the loose brains wouldn't revolt against them.

BARNEY: If it weren't for the goddamned idiocies of the tight brains, we wouldn't have had either war *or* revolutions.

JOEY: Or maybe evolution?

LEV: It is possible that, with such unnatural beings as men, change cannot come about without blood. People do not really want change. They are told by a minority that they must have it, and then a minority fights for it—and the majority are changed.

[189]

ANNIE: For the better?

JOEY: My God, if we didn't think so what's the use of anything?

LEV: But why should change always be for the better? Now more people have more access to more things than ever before, but this same accessibility to all by all has destroyed the most desirable *things* of all—peace, privacy, wilderness— the beauty of cities and the beauty of land. . . .

K: For you, Lev, or us, maybe. But is this what most people want? Look at life before we left it. What were They doing but obliterating space—silence—privacy—making a world of constant noise and constant movement. My God, that phrase— "Where the action is"!

JOEY: Didn't you want action when you were young?

K: Not necessarily. Until I was eighteen I wanted long dreaming—mostly alone.

JOEY: She's a loose brain.

BARNEY: You know where the tight brains are. They're in the business section of the newspapers. Y'know, "Mr. Fred Burpee Poop has been made Vice President of Southern Tool and Screw," and you see this smooth face with a sort of little smile, good old Fred, pillar of society, never made a false move, loves his Mum, got a darling house on Maple Lane and a frigid wife in the PTA. Boy, is his mind tight. You couldn't push an idea into it with a crowbar!

LEV: So you would prefer the dirty disciples with tattooed chests?

K: Neither may exist any more.

JOEY: Hell, Kate, as long as there's free enterprise you'll have Fred Poop, and I'll bet They've cleaned up the beards by now. . . .

At this point our clean beard, Michael, came and kneeled before Barney with what appeared to be a new drawing.

Barney looked at it, frowned, bent closer.

In almost a whisper he said, "Talk about 'tight'. . . ." And then, "Mike—much too small—what's happened to your line?" He gestured with his hands. "Open up, kid! Open up!"

Michael looked at him as if he, Barney, hadn't understood. Barney passed the drawing to Annie, then each of us saw it in silence.

It was an almost blank sheet of paper. At the very top— thinly, almost microscopically, drawn—were two curving faint lines that might have meant a road, and between them—no larger than a small beetle—a tiny, white panel truck.

■ A change in the weather has made us all feel better. I suppose you could call it a remission . . . of the disease of fear that had infected us all.

After a week of fog, which smothered the house and pressed down on our minds and lungs and hearts, a wind has finally blown in a night of rain and, veering northward, a day of clarity so pure and cool and splendid that the world seems washed.

The strip of sea is that hard dark blue, the privet leaves are polished, blades of grass shine like knives, and you can see the farthest rise of land five miles away. The air is a privilege.

But the nights are now growing cold, and the allowances for fuel have dwindled drastically. Over the years we have learned to live during winter days in a temperature never above sixty-two or -three, and by night with less, and I think we have been the better for it. It has forced us to be physically active and to rely on the miraculous adaptability of the internal thermostat instead of on the high artificial "comfort levels" of technology that we were used to before.

But what we cannot seem to do without in cold weather is the open fire, a luxury we have been allowed simply because it is the only source of heat in the house aside from two primitive gas floor heaters in the crawl space. We have no cellar.

When Jeff was alive we burned driftwood which we found on the beach and which, with the boys, we carried home in a wooden cart and later by Jeep.

But already in our last year here together we found less and less timber, why we never knew. It might have been a newly formed reef that kept it from coming in, it might have been part of that strange mystical pattern of withdrawal that I wrote of before: the sea was no longer giving us such treasure. The beaches were bare.

What we used instead was a kind of pressed pulp made out of waste into blocks or briquettes. It burned very quickly, without the aroma or sparks or physical irregularity of wood, and the amount we could buy at the Center allowed us—now—only an hour or so of fire each night. At least, that is what we figured our careful consumption of the allotted supply to be.

But now, suddenly, we decided not to hoard. Nobody said anything, nobody discussed it, but on these first cool autumn nights Joey or Lev would keep a fire going after dinner until the last one of us would go to bed. If the blocks ran out, they ran out, and we knew then what we could do.

So last night, around it, we (even Barney, who seemed better) went back to something one of us had said—when? it no longer matters—about how we had survived as a community and could not have survived as a family.

JOEY: It was about us being like Them—the kids.

LEV: Yes, I remember that charming little table of analogies that Kate drew up. We were really old Hippies, we were living a communal life—in a rather cold pad, not so?

K: I think the implication was that the whole business of the small family unit was dying out—that the young were rejecting it in favor of communal life.

JOEY: They were rejecting boring family life.

LEV: Mine was not boring.

K: Well, maybe we were lucky. None of us were brought up in middle-class suburbs with neat little houses and neat little lawns and the men away all day. This is no life. There just isn't enough *to* it.

JOEY: Look, in a family everybody knows everybody too well. By the time you're eight you could write the script yourself —what Daddy will say, what Mommy will say, and how Sis picks her nose.

BARNEY: What the hell's the difference with us? I could write every one of Lev's lectures!

LEV: No you could not. Your vocabulary is too limited.

K: Okay, so we knew each other pretty well, maybe too well, but still we each have separate underlays of experience to draw on which keep sending up new signals—surprises, even now. If we were all related to each other, if we had all shared the same blood, the same background, the well would long since have dried up and we'd just be reduced to the small talk of endless habit.

LEV: The well dries up in old marriages too.

JOEY: How old? My well dried up in five years, first time 'round.

K : It's insane to expect two people to stay together when they have nothing more to say to each other.

LEV : I agree. There is nothing worse in life than living with someone whom one can no longer sleep with or talk with.

JOEY : What's more important, Maestro?

LEV : In the last analysis, talk with. I agree with Nietzsche, who had a pretty poor view of marriage. He said *"Nicht der Mangel an Liebe, sondern der Mangel der Freundschaft macht die unglucklige Ehen."*

BARNEY : Ja Ja! (That's the only German I know.)

LEV : He said it isn't the lack of love but the lack of friendship that makes unhappy marriages. He said also that marriage was devised for average people—for the majority—who are not capable either of great love or great friendship, but that it was also for a very small few who *were* capable of both love and friendship.

JOEY : So marriage is the greatest! Big deal.

K : Look, this business of friendship—*this* is what the kids missed in the family circle. The minute somebody becomes Mom and Dad or Husband and Wife, they're fixed in molds that somehow preclude friendship. They're no longer single individuals communicating freely with each other. Except in very rare families. Maybe that's why we've tolerated each other so long. Sure, we know too much about each other, but still we're not cast in any role.

JOEY : God, how I hate that word. Masculine role, feminine role.

K : Well, that's just it. That's what They were getting away from. That's what They wanted—well, fellowship in a larger community.

LEV : That's why you have gangs and wars, my dear Kate.

The tragedy of the world is that for the ordinary man the time when he reaches his fullest capacities is in the comradeship of battle. *Not* in his family, *not* with his wife or children, but in the community of survival. . . . The accompanying tragedy is that mankind has produced no community of peace except in the Church, which has isolated itself from life.

ANNIE: What about us? What about women?

K: I don't know. Something of the same thing, maybe. When they're exposed to a great challenge—something bigger than themselves or their immediate families—I guess they become capable of more than they thought they had—or were.

JOEY: I never saw a happier bunch of dames than in politics—pushing a candidate.

ANNIE: If I had been in a war, I would be a woman guerrilla.

(Barney pummeled his chest and tried to make a Tarzan roar, but ended in a coughing spasm.)

I was going to say that I thought it was harder to live than to die, but suggested instead that maybe this community should go to bed.

Annie took Barney upstairs, but then Michael came in and sat down cross-legged on the floor, smiling and expectant, so we stayed on awhile, playing Speculation.

We wondered whether in the light of a more collective society, a more communal one, They had managed to change the institution of marriage, among other things. Perhaps, by now They had gone much further than the separation of Church and State. Marriage had been reduced to a legal contract requiring a man and woman to assume responsibility for supporting their children until they were sixteen years of age but permitting them to part by mutual consent at any time after the first five years.

Conversely, the contract could be extended by mutual consent every five years ad infinitum.

Couples having more than two children would be subjected to heavy taxation, the revenue going toward nationwide community nurseries for the children of working mothers.

Prostitutes would be licensed by the state and regularly inspected by the health authorities.

No social stigma would be attached to men and women living together out of wedlock provided they bore no children. If they did they would be subject to the usual marriage contract.

Abortion would be on demand and exempt from legal jurisdiction. This had become in any case irrelevant since abortion pills were now available to all women.

Between the ages of sixteen and eighteen and before entering universities, all boys and girls were required to live in working communities devoted to social services.

Military conscription was outlawed.

These last two speculations were the only ones that drew unanimous approval, although Joey liked the marriage and prostitute parts.

Lev wondered how many couples would renew their marriage contracts.

"A hell of a lot," said Joey. "The minute you know something isn't a life sentence, you relax. And if you relax, maybe you get to be friends—like that kraut of yours said, Maestro."

Michael was scratching Phu under the chin and Phu was purring like an electric generator. Lev got up and scooped him up and away from the youth and said, in a voice suddenly harsh, "Well—good night!" and strode upstairs.

With sudden and overwhelming sadness I thought of Jeff and the boys (and By) and the lost world of the past as the fire slowly flickered out, and then (why?) Michael put his hands up to cover his eyes and when he took them away his cheeks were wet.

He got up and came over and kissed my forehead and then went to his vigil outside Barney's door while Joey and I watched the last spark smolder and die.

After a silence Joey said, "Hell of a cold world . . ."

"Which?"

"Oh, the one we were making up—the one They've made."

"A lot of it made sense. It had to come."

"Maybe," said Joey. "But I'm glad I'm out of it."

Then he put his hand over mine and said in his old cocky way, "Let's renew the contract!"

At that I made a fool of myself, for the second time this week.

■ Yesterday, Michael brought in his fourth drawing of the panel truck. It is now the size of a matchbox and a third of the way from the top of the page.

You can see the A.A. on it clearly.

■ I just had a long talk with Annie. She wants to do it, now. She can't bear to watch Barney suffer any longer, she's sure that any moment now the truck will come, she wants to do it herself, for both of them.

I was torn in two. On the one hand I would have chosen the same course in her place. If you really love someone how can you watch them die, in terminal torture? On the other hand, they couldn't do it alone: it was now a question of all or none.

How could the rest of us continue our only slightly extended span without them? More than any family we were committed to each other, and their courage would be a constant reminder of our cowardice.

And what, dear God, could we do with their bodies? Though now we were virtually removed from life, we had—except for the men who had known war—been removed from intimate contact with death. What would we do with their bodies?

I begged Annie not to do anything until we all—finally—had thrashed it out together. For years, Death had been on our agenda. But like a world organization (was the UN still functioning?), the smaller issues kept crowding out the great, the substantive, issue of Life; and the ultimate answer was continually bypassed.

If only total disarmament could make nations inviolate, only common suicide could make us so.

Responsibility—grace—dignity—what were we waiting for?

Annie promised she would wait. I promised that she would not have to wait long.

■ Nobody, of course, wanted to do it. (Who would?) I talked to Lev and Joey separately, and they felt as I did. They wanted to put it off, to push it away; it was a frightful decision to make.

But the thought of letting them kill themselves while we lived on was just as repugnant. Nor could we really commit the final act without meaning, without signature. We had to leave something behind for Them besides our bodies. We had to formalize the act, to give it order and pattern. We had, finally, to mean what we said.

And first, we had to say it. All of us. Together.

■ The drawing of the panel truck, Michael's seventh so far, now takes up half the page, in the middle. The driver has a cap and head and shoulders and arms. But no face.

Each of us have pled with Michael not to make any more of those drawings. When we do, he spreads his arms and shakes his head as if to say "Will you never understand?"

But of course we do. It is just because we do that we can't bear them.

Yesterday Annie, weeping, begged him to stop it. He put his arms around her and rocked her as if she were a child, his head bent down against hers and his own eyes wet.

That night I said to Joey, "He's the angel of death. That's what Michael is. He's the angel of death. . . ."

I saw Joey starting to work up some sort of crack, but whatever it was it died on his lips.

■ We have set the party for tomorrow night.

Joey and I had a long huddle with Lev today and decided that we could not put it off a moment longer; that waiting for

Them to come was not only a total admission of defeat, of impotence, but unbearably squalid. We must simply manage a way out that had some pride and gallantry.

We would make it a celebration. Lev and Joey would play, we would have a huge fire, and we would break out the two last bottles of whiskey we had hoarded (for a "special occasion") since the allowance ran out. We would do this not only for the pleasure of it but because it was the obvious way to swallow what we had to swallow. "It's the best combination," said Joey as if he were selling a new kind of drink. "Pills and liquor wraps it up."

Lev protested that this lacked dignity, but we shouted him down.

"What'll we play?" Joey asked him, "'The Last Roundup'?"

"We can discuss that later," said Lev. "Perhaps *Orfeo*"—he hummed a passage from it—"or something out of the *St. Matthew Passion*."

I suggested that neither of these was exactly festive. We might need something more triumphant to ride on.

"More triumphant than Bach?" said Lev. "Have you learned nothing from these years?" Then, "Perhaps a chorale would be better in the circumstances: 'Jesu mein Freude'—of 'Ich ruf zu dir, Herr.' We have, after all, limited means of expression."

"Why don't we just play what we do best?" said Joey.

"We must practice," said Lev. "We haven't played for days . . ."

"For weeks," I said. I had told Joey that the silence was almost hardest to bear these days. The air was dead except for the sea's roar. And where once that had been a comfort, it was now merely a vast, impersonal, and unconsoling presence.

"What about the goddamned last Article?"

"If we are sober we will be inhibited," said Lev, "and if we are drunk we won't make any sense."

"So what?" said Joey. "We just conk out without telling these bastards what it's all about."

Lev said hadn't we been trying to do that ever since They put us here? He pointed at me. "What else has this poor woman been doing all this time?"

"Yes, I know," said Joey, "but we haven't ever really come to grips with this . . . this . . ."

"Death?" said Lev. "No, and you won't get Barney to talk about it even in a whisper."

Joey suggested that maybe we could do what we did before, about revelation. We could write what we felt more easily than speak it.

I said Barney loathed writing.

"But he can still draw . . ."

We finally decided that although it was in many ways a preposterous effort we were somehow committed to it. They could not just find us there sprawled on the floor like the victims of a gang murder. There had to be some ritual, some meaning.

I was delegated to tell Annie about this. Our statements were to be ready by tomorrow noon.

During the evening, we decided further, each would read not his own but another's. It would be easier that way; less self-conscious.

Finally Joey said what had been hanging in the air during all of this: "What about the boy?"

"He will be free," said Lev. "He is not one of us."

"To do what? Go where?"

"Look," said Joey, "we'll never know where he dropped out from or what he's tuned into. But he's sure tuned into something. He can take care of himself . . . your 'angel of death'!"

Phu came in then, tail high, and jumped into Lev's lap. And what about *him*, we thought? How would Lev do it—and when?

Lev stood up and swung Phu to his shoulder, draped around his neck. "So, Joey—to work. We have an important recital ahead of us!"

The men headed toward the piano, and I went upstairs to find Annie.

We sat on her bed in the tiny room. The door was half open and I could hear Barney's heavy breathing across the narrow hall.

"He's still asleep," she said. "He doesn't know it, of course, but I gave him a small one in a little soup. He has become so suspicious—so frightened—Kate, he refuses to die! He would rather suffer so—anything—than die!"

I said, lying, that we all felt that. And that was why we had planned a special celebration for the next night. To get our minds off it.

I said that Lev and Joey would play, that we would have a huge fire, and that we each had to contribute something—some toast, no matter what, to congratulate each other on existing.

Annie looked at me as if she didn't believe me. Then she sighed and shook her head.

"Barney won't write. He cares to live, but he doesn't *care* . . . not any more."

"We're going to break out the whiskey."

"The *whiskey?* Why?"

"Why not? It's a party. A big party."

She looked at me sharply again. "If Barney hears *that* . . ." And she smiled a little.

"Annie, he wouldn't have to write anything if he didn't want to. Maybe just a drawing, for fun. But we want something from both of you—anything at all—before tomorrow afternoon. Lev and Joey and I want to make a sort of show—a 'diversion'— out of it."

"I'll try," she said, and then put a hand on my arm. "Please— tell Michael—*please,* no more trucks. *Please!*"

I promised I would tell him.

■ Lev and Joey practiced the two Bach chorales all afternoon. They played better than ever, and I swung between grief and joy. Michael sat cross-legged on the floor listening to them, never taking his eyes off them.

Neither did Phu. Draped across the top of the piano in his usual position, his pale eyes followed Lev's fingers on the flute as if they were butterflies.

■ The house is incredibly quiet this afternoon of the party. Everybody seems to be in their rooms except Michael, who went outside early this morning.

Apparently Joey had gone out too, for he has just come in and asked whether I had seen Lev.

"We were supposed to practice again," he said, "but I can't

see him anywhere. I knocked on his door and when there wasn't any answer I opened it. Nothing but the cat sleeping on the bed."

I said he was probably on the beach. Joey nodded.

"Mind if I play?" he asked, and I said I wished he would, the silence was terrible.

He sat down at the piano and very softly played some of his own songs and those of others.

During this I heard the front door open and Lev come in, and I got up to greet him but stopped when I saw his face. I had never seen it that way since Lily left: a pattern of grief like a Greek mask of tragedy, all sagging lines and hollow sockets.

He went straight upstairs. Some time later—maybe an hour or so—I saw him go out again with a bundle or box under his arm. I spoke to Joey about this afterward and he had a strange troubled look on his face . . . the "worried ape" look.

"Seen Phu?" he said finally.

"Not this morning. But you said he was . . ."

"Asleep. Upstairs . . ."

"Oh my God, Joey . . . you think . . . ?"

He said nothing but turned and went upstairs, coming down again much more slowly.

"Nothing on the bed," he said. "Poor goddamn bastard."

Joey's standard obituary . . .

■ It was late afternoon before I extracted their contributions for the evening and typed them out. I deliberately did not think of what I was typing. I didn't want to. I didn't want to because I was hopelessly torn in my mind between an immense

relief at the end of long labors and a stubborn refusal to believe
in an end. But you will see *that* in writing too.

You? Who?

■ Annie was the first to bring in her toast. She had called it
What I Would Like to be Next and insisted that she read it
aloud later herself. She seemed clearly embarrassed, said she
never could write, and hurried out immediately after she
dropped it on my desk.

> What I would like to be next is very beautiful and very
> free, like a man. I would like to be a prostitute sometimes
> and a good wife others.
>
> I would like to be very educated so that I knew what I
> meant.
>
> I would like to be twenty again and start with Barney.
>
> I would like more than anything to be a great singer.
> But then I could not live with Barney, and that is what I
> really want.
>
> For now.
>
> You are all my family and I love you.
>
> Thank you.

Underneath this handwritten statement was a sheet of paper
with Barney's entry.

It was a very bold ink drawing—one of his best, I thought—of
Michael.

His naked figure, with great black wings outstretched,
towered above—hovered over—a miniature replica of this house.

Underneath Barney had scrawled *Swing Lower, Sweet
Chariot*

Joey came later with his, very sheepish. "You'll throw up," he said. "It's cheap, like me." He also said he would play and sing it: the music came easy.

> Listen—never say die,
>   The game's not over—
> We'll meet again someday
>   My lover.
>
> Listen—we'll meet again,
>   The day's not done—
> Another moon will rise,
>   Another sun.
>
> Listen—never say when,
>   Never say how—
> When you're there—it's always
>   Now.

I smiled up at him. He shrugged, grimaced, and left.

Suddenly I remembered something. I went to a carton in the hall closet, which was full of old clippings and things I had written over the years.

I remembered a series of sonnets I had written the year before Jeff died. They were about the different kinds and stages of love, for I had felt impelled to remember what these were like before I was no longer able to know them and feel them. I had had no pretensions of being a poet, but there were times when prose would not do and when I needed the containment of a specific form.

The sonnets were in a green folder, so I found them quite soon in the pile of stuff.

I looked for one particular one, the last of the series. It was the second one of two on love in age, and when I read it again, I felt it belonged to our evening—and to Joey.

She dims the light. She cannot face the light
which shows her what she knows and must ignore
if any re-evocation, however slight,
of earlier joy and wholeness can restore
their mutual need. She must forget the feel
of her own arid skin and slacking flesh,
must clothe herself in former beauties, peel
time's insult from her, weave a tenuous mesh
of illusion around both of them with word
and tender touch. Without these loving lies,
age is a curse and nakedness absurd,
and beauty, unimaginable, dies.
She dims the light so that they both can see
their separate dreams of immortality.

But still, this was about us, not about them. Joey said I had
to leave something for them. He said, suppose your grandchildren see all this, and there's no word from you? Don't you
care about them?

So much, I said, that I can't bear to think of them.

But what—if by some miracle, I thought—they ever do see
this. What will they—what will you—think of us?

That we were grotesque, senile, indecent?

That we represented no one but ourselves—freaks, snobs, the
last remnants of privilege?

That we were pitiable, or contemptible?

I don't know.

I can only hope that there might be some connective spark
between the quick and the dead: the resurrection of a flame
that was almost extinguished when They put us out.

They? How silly the word seems now.

So if I said anything tonight it would be more a prayer than a
toast. That you fight for your humanity and dignity. That you

refuse to be bent, folded, spindled, or mutilated by any machine. That you perceive and love the nature of the universe inside and outside of yourself.

That you and we are one.

Suddenly I heard Lev and Joey practicing their Bach chorales. I went very quietly to the far end of the living room where I could watch them—Joey's back at the piano and Lev facing it. When the flute-voice part ended and I could see Lev's features, they seemed remarkably controlled. What discipline, I thought, what guts. And then I remembered what music did to good musicians—and for them.

Oh God, how beautiful it all could be—if we only knew. Knew what?

■ At about six, Joey brought me what Lev had written for the "entertainment." Lev said it was to be read by me.

I drink to the artists: those who make beauty, who unlock mysteries, who serve truth.

Artists never make wars. They are too busy making life out of the matter of their visions. Only artists are timeless. They may abhor death as the arbitrary end of their search, but they need not fear it, for what they have done of real worth lives *for* them.

We are no better people than others, but we have had better lives than most. We are the luckiest ones on earth.

So many in this world are starved while we are full. So many feel impotence while we are invested with power. So many are bound while we are free. Between the poles of arrogance and humility, between failure and triumph, we walk alone, listening to voices unheard by others.

But *our* voices are heard. And in the measure by which we love what we do, we are loved by others.

You have called me prejudiced. I am. I am prejudiced against the stupid, the brutal, the lying. I am prejudiced against those who destroy and those who appease them.

But I am for the few anywhere whose gifts set them apart as guides and leaders, who are by talent and wisdom and integrity superior. I am for the aristocratic tradition, without which no civilization can exist.

So I drink to my civilized—my immortal—friends!

■ I just told Joey he simply had to trim his beard. It isn't really a beard, it's a stubble he's been nurturing for several weeks and is still a scraggle. He knows I like beards, but only when they work.

Lev would certainly be his usual elegant self, and Annie and I had agreed—almost like conspiratorial schoolgirls—to use Barney's one remaining soft pencil for eye shadow.

I know it sounds grotesque, but it's really the only way we can do it. It is, after all, a performance.

■ Michael has just come in with his arms full of grasses and wild asters, anything he could find to fill the vases.

6 P.M. Everything is ready.

The scores of "Ich ruf zu dir" and "Jesu meine Freude" are open on the piano.

The whiskey bottles and the glasses are on the sideboard, and Lev tells me that the other things are in the cupboard below it.

The fireplace is piled high with everything that can conceivably burn, including some old broken chairs that Barney couldn't manage to fix this year, and a couple of picture frames that he told Annie he would never want.

We had agreed that we would not start drinking until the music was over. (Neither Joey nor Lev, of course, ever drank before playing, and the effect of alcohol now, after long abstinence, would be disastrous.)

We would finish off the first bottle, though, before reading our toasts, or whatever they were; and the second—the drinks heavily spiked before passing—after them.

Lev would be the bartender—he promised that he not only could—but would—do it.

Michael—who else?—would be butler.

So now all we have to do is to bathe and dress before dinner. Annie told me this morning that the prospect of liquor had so transformed Barney that he asked her to get out an old Tyrolean jacket with silver buttons that he hasn't worn for how long, and a hat with a shaving brush that went with it.

I am dressed in my best outfit, the olive green with the Chinese collar.

I will put this page on top of the others in the box on my desk and cover the typewriter. It really needs cleaning; the keys stick. Tomorrow I . . .

I am afraid of the dark.

■ Joey just came in—shaved. He said I was beautiful and it wouldn't be dark.

I am trying to believe him.

AGNUS DEI, QUI TOLLIS PECCATA MUNDI,
DONA EIS REQUIEM:
    DONA EIS REQUIEM SEMPITERNAM.

LIBERA ME, DOMINE, DE MORTE AETERNA,
IN DIE ILLA TREMENDA:
QUANDO COELI MOVENDI SUNT ET TERRA:
DUM VENERIS JUDICARE SAECULUM
    PER IGNEM.

TREMENS FACTUS SUM EGO, ET TIMEO,
DUM DISCUSSIO VENERIT,
    ATQUE VENTURA IRA.

DIES ILLA, DIES IRAE, CALAMITATIS, ET
MISERIAE, DIES MAGNA ET AMARA VALDE.

LIBERA ME, DOMINE, LIBERA.

Epilogue

Although the letter in the prologue of this book from the narrator's son 6B8953A-411-Y, clarifies some of the facts involved in it, certain elements are still unresolved: namely the final hours of the five persons involved and the subsequent whereabouts of the young man called Michael.

Whether the five older people actually committed suicide as planned *before* the conflagration we will, of course, never know. Whether the fire that destroyed them was accidental—the result of escaping sparks from too great a flame—or a deliberate act on the part of Michael is open to question. But it seems reasonable to assume that had the five been alive at the start of the fire, the instincts for self-preservation would have driven them outside, whereas their total immolation in this wooden house indicates the opposite.

As for Michael, we instituted investigations of our own after failing to elicit further information from 168359217Y. Since the date of the fire had been established, our researchers, with the cooperation of the Health and Rehabilitation Agencies, were able to check the records of all hospitals in the area to discover whether they included the admission of a youth resembling Michael on that night or on following days. Needless to say, the search was made doubly difficult by the fact that due to Michael's muteness and illiteracy he could give the authorities no name. The R.A. (the Rehabilitation Agency, which has jurisdiction over all the mentally ill, criminal or otherwise) had no records of a mute in that period, bearded or not.

These findings would give credence to the theory advanced by 168359217Y that Michael was indeed a hallucination on the part of the narrator. Yet this does not explain the fact that someone somehow left this manuscript in the hands of others, who subsequently gave it underground circulation.

The investigation then led to a campus about twenty miles from the scene of the fire. After prolonged interviewing of those students suspected by the authorities to be dissidents, none admitted having seen a mute with a beard at any time, although by their manner and their responses some impressed the interviewers as being engaged in a conspiracy of silence. They were, in fact, members of a group protesting against speech as an inhibitor of thought. Since they spent one week of every month in total silence, it would have been quite possible for Michael to join them as a new student committed to the same principles. In a campus of 75,000 this would not have caused undue notice.

The clue to Michael's identity, therefore, rests with the reader.

So does a final irony. The present government, under massive pressure from the generation now in its forties—deprived of their past and fearful of their future—had repealed the age-segregation law a few weeks before these exiled five committed their last act.

The Editors

J46